PRAISE FOR THE SAILOR'S GENESIS

Have you read the prequel short story,
The Night in Lover's Bay?

See how Marcella met the crew of *Eik* and started on
her adventure. It's available to subscribers of my
newsletter for free. Sign up and get your copy at
lizalden.com.

Also by Liz Alden:

The Love and Wanderlust Series
The Night in Lover's Bay (prequel short story)
The Hitchhiker in Panama
The Sailor in Polynesia
The Chef in the Mediterranean (Fall 2021)

THE SAILOR IN POLYNESIA

A LOVE AND WANDERLUST NOVEL

LIZ ALDEN

THE SAILOR IN POLYNESIA

ISBN-13: 978-1-954705-04-3

Published by Liz Alden

Proof Edition

Cover Design by E Stokes Creative

Developmental Editor: Tiffany Tyer

Copy Editor: Kaitlin Severini

Proofreader: Annette Szlachta

To our subscribers.

And to the women who adventure alone.

CONTENT WARNING

This book contains references of past physical and emotional abuse.

And sex. There's always sex.

ONE

MY LIFE COULD HAVE BEEN A BAD MOTIVATIONAL poster.

Paradise or purgatory? It all depends on your attitude.

Right now my attitude sucked. I paced inside my boat in the late morning, trying to pick something to do, but nothing sounded good to me: snorkeling, walking on the beach, reading. Can you burn out doing relaxing things?

The most I can stand my own company is four weeks and two days, apparently. At least Liam wasn't here with me. My teeth ground just thinking about what my ex-husband would say.

But why do I need an ex-husband here to tell me these things? Liam had worked his way so far under my skin that I could hear his voice regardless: *You'll never be able to do this on your own.*

What an idiot I was. People are *the worst*.

Except for my brother James. He was the best. Speaking of which . . .

I grabbed my satellite device, a small rectangle that connected to my phone and allowed me a bare minimum of communication—because people suck, right?—and turned it on.

It took forever to boot up and get a signal, but I typed out a message to my little brother.

Hello from paradise.

James was most likely at work, so I didn't expect a response right away. But only a few moments later my phone pinged with a new message.

Hallelujah, she lives. I was going to send you a message soon to check to make sure you were alive. I was writing your obituary. Mia Walsh: great sailor, until she fell off the face of the earth AND NEVER CALLED HER FAMILY.

I rolled my eyes. *I'm alive. How are you?*

Same old, same old. I noticed your dot hasn't moved in a while.

James was referring to the GPS tracker I had on board that uploaded my location.

That's because I haven't moved in a while.

What's so interesting that's kept you there for so long?

Looking out my window, I wondered the same thing. My boat lolled at anchor in an atoll named

Kauehi, in French Polynesia. Under my keel was crystal-clear blue water and in front of me, a sandy beach with palm trees and coconuts. There were no real buildings, no people living here, no one around for miles.

Off to my starboard side lay large columns of coral, which I'd snorkeled countless times. I knew the grooves of the brain coral better than the back of my own hand, the docile black-tipped sharks had been named, and I knew which coconut trees had the sweetest nuts.

It is really beautiful.

Riiiiight. Every place you visit is really beautiful. Why are you there in that one particular harbor?

I didn't want to tell James that this was the site of one of the biggest fights that Liam and I had ever had. I had sailed here thinking that I could erase a bad memory and make myself magically better, but so far I just felt lonely.

It didn't help that the other boats that came through here were all couples. Happy couples, sailing from island to island together, popping in to say hi to poor little ole me. I couldn't deal with it and was now actively trying to avoid people.

James got impatient when I took too long to answer, and my phone chimed again.

Is there anyone else there?

LIZ ALDEN

A few boats have come and gone, but it's still early in the season. So, no, mostly I'm all by myself.

I worry about you all alone.

I'm fine, really.

But are you happy?

I should be happy, right? I thought. I was in a beautiful place, doing exactly what I wanted to be doing. It was just me and my sailboat, *Welina*, setting off to explore the world.

My phone pinged again.

It's okay if you aren't happy. You can sell Welina *and come home.*

Don't say things like that! You'll hurt her feelings!

Hers or yours?

Ouch.

Tough love, Miamati.

Miamati was the nickname Dad had given me because I was a high-energy tomboy, always running around like a Maserati. James slipped into using my nickname when he worried too much about me.

I'm fine, I swear. It's an adjustment period. Don't you have work to be doing?

Right, I'M the family slacker. ;)

That's me, professional bum.

You're only a professional if you are earning money. When are you going to post another video?

4

Geez, this is why I never message you! All it is is work work work.

It comes from a place of love. And don't think I missed you avoiding my questions. But you are saved by the bell —I have to run to a meeting. I'll give the 'rents a hug from you. Love you!

Love you too, Sir James.

Just to spite my brother, I stripped off my clothes and leaped into the water next to my boat. *I'll show you fun.*

———

IT WASN'T THAT I DIDN'T HAVE THINGS TO DO. THERE was *always* work to be done on a boat: small repairs that needed to be made and regular maintenance to keep her in good condition.

There was also a big decision that I was putting off: money.

My divorce had left me with meager savings, *Welina*, and the only remaining revenue stream in my failed marriage: a moderately successful sailing vlog.

Liam had easily turned the vlog over to me. He had hated it toward the end, but I thought he would fight for it, just to be contentious.

Welina, I had to fight for, which made my blood pressure rise just thinking about it. I was the sailor, not Liam. This whole trip had been my idea. I doubted he would ever set foot on a sailboat again.

The solution to my money woes should have been easy: publish a new video. It was not so simple.

Last week I'd motored over to the closest village, ten miles across the lagoon as the crow flies. Man could not live on bread alone, but a diet of nothing but coconuts wasn't going to work either, and the little village was my best choice.

Watching myself on camera used to be so much easier. I pulled up a clip I'd filmed during the trip and hit play.

My long red hair was up in a ponytail, and the wind caused it to whip around behind me like a whirlwind. I stood at the helm, the island a narrow strip of land behind me.

"I've just left Tiera . . . Teava . . ."

On-camera me took a deep breath and started again.

"I've just left Tearavero, the village on the atoll of Kauehi. You can see it behind me." I held up a finger and pointed over my shoulder. *"I've gotten some provisions, but there's not much. I was able to trade for some fish, which was nice. Since it's just me"*—my voice wobbled here—*"and there are tons of sharks in the Tuamotus, spearfishing is definitely not a good idea, so I,*

ah, need to rely on trading with fishermen or canned food for protein."

I hit the pause button and closed my eyes. It didn't feel like me anymore. I looked uncomfortable, and it wasn't just the missing dynamic of a second person. The feeling weighed on me all the time, this lingering idea that Liam had ingrained in me that I wasn't good enough.

Double-clicking on another video, I watched myself again.

"It's a real privilege to be spending all this time in Kauehi. There have been other boats passing through while I've been here. Right now I'm all alone." I panned around behind me, showing the empty waters around the boat.

"Sailboats coming through the South Pacific tend to stop for a few nights because it's so beautiful. But most sailors are on a timeline to get through the islands before cyclone season starts, and since I'm going to store Welina *in Apataki again, I don't have far to go. So my neighbors usually move on after a few nights."*

The clip ended on my face and *God*, I looked haggard. I didn't want to use any of this footage. How was I going to keep myself afloat without my videos?

———

LATER, I PORED OVER A COOKBOOK, TRYING TO FIND some inspiration for cooking with the meager supplies I had. It might be time to go into town again.

My thoughts were interrupted by an unfamiliar sound.

Living on a boat, I tried to attune myself to unusual noises. An unfamiliar banging of my sails? Might be chafing. Engine making a racket? Might have a blockage.

Blinking, I wiped the sweat off my brow and tilted my head, trying to listen for the noise again.

Clang clang clang . . .

I sat bolt upright.

"Are you fudging kidding me?" I said to *Welina.* "Square miles of beautiful water and someone is anchoring right next to us?"

I scanned the view around me and located the offender. Okay, they weren't anchoring *that* close to me, but I was still irritated anyway.

My new neighbor was big and beautiful. At least, bigger than my home, *Welina,* the forty-five-foot Morgan sailboat. I recognized the lines: she was an Oyster, maybe fifty-five feet long. A young woman stood at the bow while the anchor chain clanged against the roller, dropping the anchor to the sand beneath the boat's keel.

A man walked along the deck on the port side, hands passing from one part of the rigging to another as he weaved his way aft toward the cockpit. He was young too: tanned and shirtless, looking a bit scruffy, as cruisers were wont to do.

When he reached the woman on the bow, he slid behind her and gripped her hips affectionately. Together, they bent down and mussed with the anchor chain.

I bit my lip. Were they the owners or crew? It was rare to see young people cruising. I was thirty-five and I hardly ever met people my own age. Most cruisers were older: retired, or in early retirement. The quality of the boat made the crew category more probable; I'd met a few Oysters, and they almost always had crew.

The boat drifted back as her anchor dropped, her bow swinging to port, making it hard for me to see the cockpit. As the weight of the boat fell back onto the anchor, she aligned more with the wind and came to sit parallel to me, about a hundred feet off *Welina*'s starboard side.

Now I could see the helmsman. He was also young and shirtless, with a shock of nearly white hair pulled back into a small ponytail. He stood at the center cockpit, his hands on the wheel, one foot on the seat next to him. A big Norwegian flag flew off the stern of the boat.

My eyes lingered on the guy at the helm for a moment. I liked the way he held himself. He was relaxed and calm, definitely confident in his boat, his crew, his skills. I wished for a little of that confidence for myself. I used to have it. How could I get it back?

"Oh, poor *Welina*. Beautiful new boat, gorgeous young people on board." I patted the canvas Bimini over the cockpit. "We're a little scruffier, but we're made of tough stuff, right?"

While I watched, another head popped up from the companionway. A tanned dark-haired woman entered the cockpit and surveyed the landscape.

She took in one of my favorite views in the whole world, and I tried to look at it through her eyes and remember what it was like the first time I sailed here, the first time I dropped anchor with the beach a hundred yards off my bow, coconut trees thick from one side of the motu to the other.

All this was fresh and new to these sailors.

I focused back on my new neighbors and found them looking at me. I also realized I was sprouting bitch wings—hands on hips, elbows cocked out— while I watched them, which wasn't the friendliest thing to do. My hands fell to my sides.

And of course, my new neighbors waved.

I gave them a stiff wave back and decided maybe if I made myself scarce, they'd get the idea that I wasn't interested in being chatty. I ducked into the companionway of *Welina* and gave my idle hands some busywork.

TWO

WELINA WAS AN EXCELLENT PLACE FOR HIDING. AND also for being a creeper. Or *spy*, if you wanted to sound fancy.

I watched my new neighbors from the windows of my salon, confident no one could see me in the porthole. They were too busy to notice me anyway.

The two from the bow were obviously a couple. They'd puttered around tidying the boat up, staying close to each other, and I could hear their occasional laughter drift over. The tanned brunette had disappeared below, so that left me watching the skipper.

Which was the best option of all. This guy was tall and lean, and he'd bent to work inflating a stand-up paddleboard. I could barely see what he was doing, but I was curious about what brand of paddleboard it was. I could barely make out an *a* and a *p*.

Binoculars were helpful. Yes, I could definitely read the name of the paddleboard company now.

There was a lot of muscle flexing going on. I'd never inflated a stand-up paddleboard before—I always wanted one, and nearly had a sponsor give me one, but I had to back out—so I didn't know how hard it was, but based on the way this guy's muscles were moving, it was quite a workout.

I nibbled my lip. I might have been a bit deprived lately.

Once the board was inflated and pushed into the water, I watched the man climb down and stabilize himself. The brunette came out of the boat and handed him . . . something. I couldn't tell what it was. He placed it on the board between his feet and pushed off his boat.

And pointed directly at me.

"Oh crap," I muttered. Still peeking through the binoculars, I watched him paddle toward me, strong arms stroking a few times on each side before switching. I shook myself: time to stop peeping before he gets close enough to notice.

———

"*HALLO?*" A MAN'S VOICE CALLED OUT.

I stepped into the cockpit and looked toward the

starboard side. At the gunwale a few feet away, strong fingers gripped the rail, and a moment later a blond head popped up. His hair was pulled back in a bun, his skin tanned and eyes hidden behind sunglasses.

When he saw me, his eyebrows rose and his mouth fell open.

"Uhhh . . . hi," I called back, not moving from my cockpit.

He stared at me briefly and then shook himself. "Yes, I have . . . I have a gift for you." He had a thick accent that must have been Norwegian, and his fingers twitched nervously on the rail.

Despite the minor annoyance of my busy afternoon being interrupted—naps were important—I was intrigued. Who came bearing gifts to total strangers?

Reaching down, he lifted the gift, a fillet of tuna in a plastic bag. "We . . . we caught this on the way here from Rangiroa, and even though there are five of us on board . . ." He trailed off and his mouth opened and closed a few times.

"That looks like tuna?" I supplied.

For whatever reason, he hastily started opening the bag and then tried to pull out the fish.

"You don't have to . . ."

In doing so, he let go of *Welina* and started to drift

away. When he noticed, he lunged for the gunwale again, throwing himself off balance. I watched in horror as he, and the tuna fillet, plunged into the water.

I scrambled to my knees. His boat had just come in, he may not know . . .

"Get out, get out, get out," I chanted as he surfaced, the tasty morsel of tuna bobbing next to him. "Sharks swim around here all the time."

His sunglasses were gone, so I saw his eyes widen. Thankfully, he was still tethered to the paddleboard, so he turned and grabbed it, lunging to climb on.

I saw the moment he made the decision, but I could only watch in horror as he swept his hand through the water and scooped up the tuna.

Safe on his knees on the paddleboard, he panted and rubbed his hands over his face. He cursed in Norwegian.

"Are you okay?" I asked.

He held up one hand and pinched the bridge of his nose with the other. "I know—I should not have done that."

"Which part? The falling in or the scooping up?" I teased, trying to lighten the mood.

He laughed darkly.

"Why don't you come on board? I'll put the tuna

away and if you need a shot for fortitude, I've got tequila."

He smiled weakly without meeting my eyes and then paddled over. I helped him up and when I turned to follow him into my boat, a shadow in the water caught my eye.

I only made it a few steps before I ran into his back. He stood at the bottom of the stairs, his eyes tracking all around the salon. I cleared my throat, and he shook himself as he moved out of the way.

"So you arrived from Rangiroa?" I asked, fishing out the bottle of tequila from the cabinet. There were only a few inches left in the bottle, but I waggled it at the man anyway.

He swallowed and nodded. My muscles still felt jumpy and quivery, the adrenaline working through my system, and I hadn't even been the one in the water. I fished out two clear plastic tumblers—cloudy with age and remnants from *Welina*'s previous owners—and sloshed a finger of tequila into each one.

"Cheers." I offered up my glass, and he clinked his with mine and quickly tossed the tequila back. With his chin raised, the long column of his throat throbbed as he swallowed, and I turned my attention to my glass. I wasn't a big tequila drinker, but sometimes it was called for.

I tossed mine back too, grimacing.

Then I busied myself with the tuna, chopping it, sealing it, and putting it in my fridge. My guest stood in the center of the cabin, his gaze flitting around. I saw the guy run his hands over his face and then he actually . . . laughed?

When he caught me watching him, he broke into a smile that lit up his whole face. "I cannot believe I am here. This is surreal. You always filmed your outros in that corner"—he pointed to the couch with the globe behind it—"and I remember there used to be a heater in here that you ripped out."

"Ooooooh," I said, realization dawning on me. "You've watched my videos."

While it was true that in the whole scope of the internet, my little sailing videos were moderately successful, one of the unexpected pleasures of making videos was how *passionate* the audience was.

When Liam and I had left *Welina* in Apataki and flown home to Seattle, we had thrown a little meet and greet. It was our first "public" event, and we walked into the bar thinking that there was an office happy hour or something going on, but no. It had all been for us. People had taken time out of their lives to come meet us, and in some cases they'd even driven up from Portland.

We had spent the entire night talking with like-minded people, fellow sailors or future sailors who had watched our videos and learned from us. I'd left feeling energized and nostalgic to get back to the boat, something I desperately needed at the time.

So I was, in a sense, mildly famous, and I had an enthusiastic—and nervous—fan on board.

"Yes!" he said. "They were amazing. You did a great job with them."

"Well, thank you." I held out my hand. "I'm Mia."

"*Ja*, I know." He grinned and shook my hand enthusiastically.

I leaned in and stage-whispered, "That's my way of asking what your name is."

He laughed and palmed his forehead, pulling his hand away. "Ah, of course. Jonas."

Standing in *Welina*, he made the space look small. He must have been around six feet tall and he towered over me as he carefully made his way around the boat, ducking slightly to protect his head.

Jonas looked around the boat and I braced myself, expecting him to ask about Liam. Instead he turned around and gave *Welina* a once-over. "She looks good. You have worked hard on her," he said approvingly.

"Thank you," I said. "She was hauled out for nearly a year, and it was tough to have the boat out of the water for so long, especially one that shows her age like *Welina*."

His eyes turned to me and they were startlingly blue. "You have not made a video in a while."

"Right. Well . . ." I let my words trail off, not knowing how to explain to a total stranger that I wasn't very inspired to create anything right now. I finally went with: "I don't have any internet out here."

He nodded, accepting my answer. "How long have you been here?"

"A few weeks. I saw a few people on your boat. Are you the owner or crew?"

"*Eik* is all mine. My brother is with me, his girl-friend, and two other crew members."

I raised my eyebrows. "That's a pretty full boat."

He chuckled. "Some days it feels more full than others."

"Well, thank you for the tuna," I said, and his face fell.

"Ja, of course." He hesitated before climbing up the companionway and into the cockpit, with me following closely behind. Before he could climb down onto his paddleboard, he stopped and palmed the back of his neck. "How much longer will you be staying here?"

I shrugged. "I'm not sure yet. I don't have any plans."

"Okay." He hesitated and looked out at his boat. "If you need anything . . ."

"Thanks," I said. "Same for you, being neighbors and all."

I helped Jonas climb onto his board and then waved goodbye while he paddled away. Most boats that had passed through here only stayed a night or two. It was unlikely that *Eik* would linger, so soon I'd be alone in the anchorage again.

I needed to get better at entertaining myself.

THREE

THE NEXT DAY, THERE WAS A KNOCK ON THE SIDE OF THE hull, and the voice that accompanied it was not Jonas's. Instead a woman called out, "Hello!"

Coming out of the cockpit, I looked left and right. There was no one.

"Hello?"

"Over here." I peered down the side of the deck and found a young woman sitting on her knees on a paddleboard. "Sorry, mate, I'm not as good with the board as Jonas is." She had a light Australian accent, a mess of brown curls pulled back into a ponytail, a sunburned nose, and a pair of sunglasses protecting her eyes.

"Mia, right? I'm Lila, from *Eik*. Eivind's girlfriend."

"Eivind?" I waved Lila in and she climbed up.

"Yes, Jonas's brother. I'm here on a super-special international relations mission." Lila wriggled her eyebrows.

"Oh?"

"Yes, can we borrow some sugar?"

I laughed. "Sure, come on in."

Lila followed me into *Welina*. "How long have you been here in Kauehi?"

"A little less than a month," I called back over my shoulder. My galley was to the right at the base of the stairs, so I turned in and opened cabinets to pull out the container. Lila stood in the center of the salon, looking around. My cheeks burned a little bit; *Welina* was not looking her best right now. I'd tried to tackle a project this morning rebuilding an old pump, but it wasn't going well. Clutter was everywhere and, not expecting company, I had left the project strewn about the main salon.

Lila's lips pursed and I braced for a comment, but instead she climbed onto the couch. There was a half-wall between the salon and the galley, and she kneeled on the seat and leaned over to watch me pour some sugar into a baggie.

"So," she started. "Jonas came back from saying hello yesterday completely soaking wet. What happened?"

"He didn't tell you?"

"Yeah, no. He just kind of mumbled something, wouldn't meet my eyes, and disappeared into his cabin."

I grinned despite myself. "Well, he scared the crap out of me. He was giving me the tuna fillet"—I looked up and she nodded—"and he fell in the water *with* the fillet."

"Oh my God!" Lila shrieked. "There are so many sharks here. Thank God he didn't get bitten."

"I know. And we're so far from medical care too. I do not want to be attempting to stitch up a shark bite."

Lila rolled her eyes. "The irony. Of all of us, Jonas is the one I would want to stitch up my shark bite. I'm going to stay the hell out of the water."

I finished zipping up the bag and raised my hands. "It's not a big deal. Normally they won't bother you at all. Just don't dump fish guts overboard and jump immediately in the water. That's just asking for it."

She shuddered. "Where I come from, shark attacks are a serious deal!"

"Aussie, I'm guessing?"

"Yes! A shark ate our prime minister once, thank you very much." She paused. *"Allegedly."*

I handed her the bag of sugar. "Are you going to be okay paddling back to your boat?"

"Nah, yeah. Probably." She looked thoughtful. "Hopefully. I'm kind of new to the paddleboarding thing."

"Well, I do have a dinghy, but it's pretty heavy and really hard to get up and down by myself. But we can call your boat on the radio if they are listening?"

"That's okay. Thanks, though." She took a step toward the companionway and then hesitated. "Listen, based on the whole falling-in-the-water thing, and the way Jonas is behaving back on our boat . . ."

My brows rose. "How is Jonas behaving on your boat?"

Lila placed a hand on my arm in reassurance. "Jonas is not himself right now. I don't watch sailing vlogs, so I, like, don't understand your fame and whatnot, but he's excited and clearly way too enthusiastic. I promise, he's a nice guy. He's just . . . fangirling?"

I tried to hide a smile behind my hand, but Lila caught it.

"I know, it's hard to picture a six-foot-tall hardy Norwegian man fangirling, but he is."

"I mean . . . it was kind of adorably dorky?"

"Well, get ready for more adorable dorkiness. Come over for dinner tonight. I promise I'll act as a buffer and calm him down if he gets to be too much, but by the end of the night I bet we can get him to be his normal, charming self."

"Ah, I don't know . . ."

"Well, Marcella, our chef, insists, since you're giving us sugar."

A grin tugged at my lips. "You have a chef?"

Lila sniffed and stuck her nose up in the air, a teasing glint in her eye. "Yes, *Eik* is serving the hottest cuisine this side of Tahiti. You would be remiss if you ignored my invitation. Tonight will be *the* party in the lagoon."

I giggled. "All right, count me in."

"Good. You saved our captain from near death. We owe you."

I escorted Lila back out on deck. "Your paddle-board is cool."

"I know, right? I've only used it a couple of times, so I need to get more practice in. Do you have one?"

I shook my head. "I wish. It would make my life a bit easier right now, but it was the last thing on my mind when I was getting ready for the season."

Lila carefully stepped down onto the board and lowered herself to her knees. "We have two. Maybe once I get the hang of it, we can go for a paddle together. But for now, I've got to get this sugar to Marcella. Thanks, Mia!"

––––––––––

At five o'clock sharp I heard an outboard fire up. I grabbed a plate of cheese and crackers I'd made and went on deck to greet my ride as Jonas pulled up alongside *Welina*.

We exchanged little smiles and I sat on the edge of the boat. He wiped his hand on his shirt nervously and then offered it to help me down into his dinghy.

I slid my palm into Jonas's, braced for the drop down, and slipped off the deck. The dinghy rocked and my momentum pushed us together, our chests brushing.

Jonas caught my waist with a firm grip and gave me a shy smile. "Hi."

"Hey," I said back, a blush rising at his proximity. "Thank you for having me over." We stepped apart and I settled onto the tube.

He nodded and focused on driving us over to *Eik*, a fast and quiet ride.

Eik was filled with music and laughter, quite the contrast. I climbed aboard—using Jonas's firm grip to help me again—and followed him onto the boat.

"Mia!" Lila cried out when she saw me. "Welcome to *Eik*. Oh, you brought something; that's so nice of you."

I shrugged. "Honor among thieves, right? We

may be seaward vagabonds, but at least we have our social niceties."

Lila laughed and led me by the elbow. Jonas's brother Eivind, broader, but with the same light hair and blue eyes, sat at the main salon table rolling meat and cheese and stabbing them with skewers. Lila took the plate of cheese and crackers from me. "Eivind, this is Mia. I think you can stop rolling nibbles now."

Lila's boyfriend tossed the skewer aside and collapsed back. "Thank God." He smiled and leaned forward to offer me a cheek. We kissed on both sides and Lila spun me around.

"Marcella," she called out. "Here is your sugar fairy godmother." Marcella oversaw two pots in the kitchen, a wooden spoon in one hand and a potholder in the other. Her hair was dark and long, spilling over her shoulders and accenting her olive complexion.

"Benvenuto," she said, and we kissed cheeks too.

"I'm lucky to have her," Lila stage-whispered. "You should see what the boys cook when they give Marcella a night off." Lila shuddered dramatically.

Marcella rolled her eyes. "Those boys. I'm a professional chef," she explained. "And thank you for the sugar." Marcella's accent was light and sultry.

She was a little bit older than the rest of the crowd, more in my age group than the others'.

"I don't know what I'm going to do when you're gone," Lila moaned.

Marcella grinned and patted her head. "You'll be my little sous chef until then; I will teach you not to starve."

Lila focused her attention back on me. "Elayna is the last of our group—I think she's back in her room still. Oh, we have a special treat for you." She turned us both until we found Jonas standing in the corner. His eyes immediately snapped to mine and he shifted uncomfortably.

"Jonas, offer her the drink." She elbowed him and gave me a wink.

Jonas licked his lips and ran a hand through his hair. It was loose now, the blond strands grazing his shoulders. "I, ah . . . I got you something. While I was onshore."

He pulled open a drawer in the galley once Marcella was out of the way, and reached in and pulled out a husked coconut, the pale fibers roughly cut. Jonas blushed and held it out to me.

My heart melted a little bit. "Aw, that's so sweet. They're my favorite."

"Ja," he mumbled.

Lila stifled a giggle behind her hand.

Marcella peeked over Jonas's shoulder. "Take that outside and open it for her." She passed Jonas a chef's knife. "Careful!" she called out to him as he climbed up the stairs. She craned her neck and caught sight of the sky. "Actually, all of you outside; it's almost sunset time."

"Sunset time, Elayna!" Lila yelled toward the front of the boat.

We gathered up drinks and platters and napkins and trooped upstairs. *Eik*'s cockpit was spacious, so much bigger than mine, and filled with stuffed pillows and cushions. I took a seat in the aft corner, out from under the Bimini so I could see the sky. Instead of raising the table in the middle, Lila climbed up behind me, where the back of *Eik* was flat and wide-open. Eivind tossed her some pillows and a beach blanket, and she made a nest on the deck.

"This is where we lie to stargaze," she told me. The platters of snacks went between us, and Lila and Eivind lay down on their stomachs.

Elayna appeared at the top of the stairs. She was willowy, with dishwater-blond hair and a bohemian style that Frenchwomen always pulled off so effortlessly.

She offered me her hand and a brittle smile, her eyes taking my measure.

"So, you are the sailor girl we hear so much about

from Jonas." She had a thick French accent and the way she said Jonas's name was much smoother than my American tongue could handle.

"Yes, Mia. Nice to meet you."

Marcella came up the stairs with a drink in one hand and a reusable straw in the other. Jonas returned from the stern and wordlessly offered me the coconut. He'd skillfully cut a square out of the top. Marcella dunked the straw in, and I gripped the coconut with both hands. Looking up, I caught Jonas's eye. "Thanks for the coconut. That was thoughtful of you."

He ducked his head and sat in the corner across from me. Marcella sat beside me, kicking her feet up on the center console, while Elayna sat next to Jonas, tucking her feet delicately underneath her and resting her elbow on the back of the bench. She gave a melodramatic sigh and touched Jonas's cheek lightly with her fingers. "You are being so shy."

Jonas blushed and swatted her away.

"Your boat is gorgeous," I offered.

He brightened immediately. "Thank you."

"How long have you had her?"

"I bought her in England, about a year and a half ago. She was built only two years ago, and had just one owner, who never took her out."

I nodded. "That's a nice find."

"Mia." Lila picked up a cheese-covered cracker. "Tell me more about your sailing channel?"

I cut my eyes to Jonas. His face flushed again and he looked away.

Lila continued. "I've never watched your channel or any YouTube sailing channel. I mean, I didn't know it was a thing before meeting Jonas and Eivind. You've been pretty successful, yeah?"

I opened my mouth to answer, but Jonas cut in. "The channel is very successful."

I snapped my mouth closed. Not *exactly* the word I would use, but okay. "Thanks," I said with a smile.

Jonas took it as permission to say more. "She has a lot of subscribers. Maybe a hundred thousand?"

"Wow, that's impressive." Lila looked at me.

"They bought the boat in California," Jonas said. I shifted a little bit at the near mention of Liam, but Jonas plowed on. "And Mia spent a lot of time working on it. She made dozens of videos of boat projects."

Lila's eyes were round when they turned back to me. "That's amazing. I have a degree in engineering, but I've discovered I'm fairly useless on a boat."

"You are not useless," Eivind chided her, and brushed a strand of hair back behind her ear.

She patted his cheek. "Liar." They grinned at each other.

Elayna leaned in for a snack and asked, "So when did you start sailing your boat?"

"We left California about two years ago." Before I could continue, Jonas butted in again.

"They sailed down the coast to Mexico, and crossed the Pacific from there, ja?"

I nodded.

"You must have done a good job with all the work on your boat, to get her out here from California," Eivind remarked.

"I guess so." I thought about my current project list. I knew logically it was shorter than in those early days, but it didn't feel like it. "It sure did take longer than we thought it would. We ended up leaving California late, and hustled to cross the Pacific, which was a disaster."

Lila chortled. "Yeah, nah, does anyone's crossing really go all that well?"

I raised an eyebrow. "You had some trouble?" I looked over *Eik*'s deck. She was sparkling clean and nearly new.

"A lot of small things, and errors on our part, made for an eventful trip," Jonas said.

"You crossed the Pacific and came here, yeah? To French Polynesia?" Lila asked.

I nodded. "We were late, and the passage had been hard and that's kind of where things fell apart, so we stored the boat over in Apataki and flew back home." I picked at the fringe on my sarong.

"And then . . ." Lila trailed off.

Ugh, the stupid *d* word.

"Liam and I got divorced," I said, averting my eyes from the sympathetic gazes. "And I kept the boat."

Lila wrinkled her nose. "So you came back alone? That must have been scary!"

"Well, to be fair, Apataki isn't far from here. I've just been puttering around a few hours at a time, hopping around the islands."

Jonas came to my defense. "Mia is an amazing sailor, and has been since she was a kid."

"Mon Dieu!" Elayna rolled her head back against the wall. "We get it—you have watched all the videos."

Jonas covered his face with his hands, his ears turning red. Lila and Eivind teased Jonas, but I didn't think Elayna was teasing. I bit my tongue to keep from coming to his defense. He wasn't the first person who'd tried to impress me with their knowledge of my videos.

"I think that's amazing." Marcella turned back to me. "There are so few women out here who are, you know, active sailors."

"Right, well, even with all this experience, people

still think you're crazy. First, we told our families we were going out sailing, and my family wasn't thrilled, but they were supportive. Liam's family was vocal about their feelings." I hesitated, not wanting to get too messy, and decided to move on. "And then, when you share your adventures online, the internet is full of the naysayers, the armchair sailors who are not afraid to tell you that you don't know what you are doing and you are going to die."

"Fuck them," said Eivind, and I surprised myself by laughing.

"Yeah, fuck them."

FOUR

THE CONVERSATION EBBED AWAY FROM MY VIDEOS AND we talked about previously visited islands and boat projects. We watched as the sun crept toward the horizon and, since we were surrounded by the atoll, celebrated the moment the top of the sun dipped below the tree line. The chorus of yips and yews echoed over the water.

Marcella disappeared back down below, waving away my offer to help in the galley. Across from me, Jonas had slipped into a relaxed slump, tilting his head back up at the sky. Elayna had leaned against him more and more, and they had defected into a side conversation. Jonas was so much more comfortable with her than he was around me. This was the first time I'd seen him relax and be less self-conscious.

Lila spoke up, turning my attention away from Jonas. "Mia, you are certainly inspiring me. I have so much to learn."

Thankful for the change in conversation, I faced Lila. "How long have you been a sailor?"

"Let's see, I joined *Eik* in Panama and we left in early March."

"Wait, so how long had you known Eivind before you agreed to sail across the Pacific on *Eik*?"

Lila wrinkled her nose. "Two weeks. I know it sounds crazy, and maybe a bit naïve, but I had a good feeling about everything. It's a good boat, and Eivind and Jonas are so different, and yet the same. They make a great team."

"How so?"

Lila rolled onto her stomach and propped her chin on her hand before answering. "They have good morals. Eivind is more of a wild child, but they are both so easygoing. Jonas would rather have peace and quiet, while Eivind's more likely to be playing music or singing or strumming his guitar. Of course, they are both devilishly handsome."

Lila pressed a kiss to Eivind's shoulder. Eivind leaned into her and took a breath before planting a chaste kiss on Lila's lips. They shared a smile that made my heart clench.

Jonas and Eivind were ridiculously handsome.

Eivind was a bit shorter and stockier than Jonas, but they both had the same light blond hair and sharp blue eyes. Jonas's limbs were long and lanky—he barely fit sitting sideways in the cockpit, both legs bent at the knee, one leg against the cushion, the other against the backrest. His feet were a few inches away from my thighs, his calves toned. Viewing his leg like this, I could see the edges of a tattoo peeking around from the back of his calf.

Was I just admiring his feet?

I think I realized it at the same time Jonas did, because I looked up to find him watching me. He held my gaze for a moment.

I flushed. "Your tattoo. Did you get it here in French Polynesia?"

Jonas grinned and twisted his leg so I could see it better. "Ja. Eivind, Elayna, and I both got tattoos in Nuku Hiva."

Eivind twisted and lifted his sleeve, showing me a large tattoo that covered his deltoid. My eyes widened. "I've heard from other cruisers about the tattoo process."

"It was amazing. The artists ask you questions, you tell them about your life and what's important to you. And they create this"—Jonas gestured to his calf—"story that is just yours."

"Did they use a tattoo gun, or the traditional method?"

"A gun," Eivind said. "The tattoo guy said that they preferred not to do tattoos for foreigners the traditional way. Which makes sense. It was a little shack, and there were not," Eivind struggled with his English, "traditional standards of hygiene, but it was the experience. And I love my tattoo."

"What about you, Lila? Did you get one?"

She shuddered. "No, I couldn't even watch Eivind's being done."

"Elayna?"

"*Oui.*" She stood up, lifting her shirt to reveal a delicate winding tattoo along her rib cage.

"Oh my God," I breathed. "That is gorgeous."

She smiled at me. "Thank you. It hurt like hell. Do you have one?"

"No, I wanted one, but Liam wouldn't let me." The words were out of my mouth before I realized what I was saying. Jonas's eyes narrowed, and I quickly tried to steer the conversation away from Liam. "Elayna, when did you join *Eik*?"

"In the Canary Islands in November. The boys rescued me from the boat I was supposed to cross the Atlantic on. The captain was a horrible drunk."

"And Marcella?"

"She joined in Antigua in January," Jonas said.

"Marcella is planning on leaving us in Tahiti, though, sadly, if she can find a job."

"Was that weird?" I asked Lila. "Coming onto a boat almost like a fifth wheel?"

"Nah. Eivind was pretty smitten with me from the get-go." She playfully nudged his side.

"I was. It took some real convincing to get you." Eivind rolled over onto Lila and then rolled back, pulling her over with him in a fit of giggles.

The uncomfortable feeling of being old sank in. Eivind and Lila were young, in their early twenties, and Jonas was, I supposed, in his late twenties. At thirty-five, I felt like the mature and responsible matron, frowning at the misbehaving youths with their whole world ahead of them.

Until Jonas poked me with his foot. I met his eyes, and he lifted a brow. "A little disgusting, no?"

I laughed. Lila and Eivind paid us no heed and continued to make kissing noises interspersed with giggles.

Jonas stood up. "Would you like another coconut? Maybe with rum this time?"

"How about a beer?"

He nodded and climbed down the stairs.

Before Jonas could come back up, Marcella announced that dinner was ready. We settled around the table, Jonas and Marcella on either side of me, and tucked into the fish she had made.

"You guys," Lila said, "the fish you caught today are nice."

"Where did you go spearfishing?" I asked.

"Out in the pass," Jonas answered. "The fish here in the lagoon are too small. These are much bigger." He settled back next to me, sipping his drink. "I have not seen you out spearfishing."

Eivind looked up. "You spearfish, Mia?"

I shook my head. "Not much anymore. Too dangerous going by myself."

"Mia is an excellent free diver," Jonas told his crew.

I blushed and shifted in my seat. I understood that I had put my life out there, publicly, but it was weird to have someone know so much about me when I knew so little about them. "Thank you," I said. "I'm out of practice now."

Lila perked up. "Eivind tried to teach me a few things about free diving, exercises to try to stay down longer, and stuff like that."

"Ja," Eivind said, nudging Lila. "We should try again now that we have nice clear water to play in."

"If you want, we can give it a go together tomorrow," I offered.

Lila perked up. "Really? That would be great! I

am not very good, obviously. Certainly not as good as Eivind or Jonas."

"Mia is even better than me," Jonas admitted.

"I don't know about that," I said. "We might have to have a little friendly competition."

"We can make a bet, ja?"

"We can bet coconuts!"

Jonas laughed. "Ja. As many coconuts as you want."

After so many weeks of being by myself constantly, it was a shock to be in the center of a close-knit group. Voices rose and people laughed. Marcella was the consummate hostess, popping up to get us anything we needed, and Eivind kept us laughing.

Elayna was quieter now, casting glances at Jonas. There was definitely something there, something in the way they interacted with each other that gave me a twinge of discomfort. Had something happened between them? Or was it just difficult crew dynamics? What would it be like to be a crew member who could be asked to leave the boat anytime?

After dinner, we stayed out in the cockpit, drinking. Since I'd been told to help myself to drinks, I went into the main salon and opened the fridge, looking for another beer. The drawer opened faster than I thought it would, and a husked green coconut rolled into view from the back.

I smiled to myself and grabbed a beer next to it.

BEFORE I LEFT, I SAID MY GOODBYES AND HUGGED everyone good night.

Lila grabbed my elbow. "What time tomorrow for free diving?"

I held my arms out wide and shrugged.

She smirked. "Nothing on the agenda, huh?"

"Another day in paradise."

Jonas drove me back to *Welina* and held on to the rail for me. I stood up and offered him a hug.

He accepted it awkwardly, wrapping one long arm around me and accentuating how short I was compared to him.

When I pulled back, he blushed. "Sorry, about everything."

"It's okay. I mean, it's kind of weird, but it's okay. You know me really well, and I'm getting to know you."

"Ja, I know." He huffed a self-deprecating laugh, and I felt a little bad for him. He was nervous, and we all handle nervousness in our own ways.

"I like the part I'm getting to know, though," I offered.

"Really?" He smiled shyly.

"Yeah." I looked back over my shoulder at *Eik*, all lit up in the darkness, the stars spread above her and laughter still echoing around. "Thank you for having me tonight. It was a lot of fun."

"You are welcome." Jonas offered me his hand and I gripped it, hoisting myself up to sit on *Welina*'s deck. Jonas might be a little awkward around me, but his grip was firm and strong. I liked it.

"Night, Jonas."

"Good night, Mia."

FIVE

THE NEXT MORNING, I WOKE UP AND LAY IN BED, listening to the soft noises of the boat sitting at anchor, willing myself to get up and make coffee. I cocked my head when I heard a soft little noise, a new noise, every time the boat rocked.

I got up to investigate, climbing out of the cockpit and looking at the starboard side. There, sitting on the deck between a stanchion and the toe rail, was a husked green coconut. This wasn't a beautiful coconut, husked with a sharp machete into a pleasing shape, the idyllic drink served at a resort on a tropical beach. This was the rough-hewn bare nut of the coconut, which rolled gently from side to side on my deck, no flat bottom to keep it upright. The boat swayed, and I watched the coconut thunk against the stanchion.

When I looked up, I saw Jonas sitting in the cockpit of *Eik*. He raised his hand in a shy little wave. I was too far away to see his face, but I had no trouble imagining pink climbing his cheeks and a bashful smile on his lips.

Why was he giving me a coconut? Was this a gift from a fan, or something different? Something more . . . personal? I picked the coconut up and ran my fingers over the coarse husk. Jonas would have intended this to be a friendly gift, from neighbor to neighbor, surely. But it meant more to me.

It was a lot of work to prepare a coconut, and one of the things I'd fought over with Liam. He had complained that they were messy, they took up too much space, and they were too much work to get open. He'd never given me one, and here I had a man I barely knew who'd given me two already, just because he knew I liked them.

It felt a little like being pampered. Even with no one here, I ducked my head, blushing. Jonas didn't know how much this sweet gesture meant to me, how it made my heart ache.

It's just a coconut, Mia.

———

I HEARD AN ENGINE START UP AND I POKED MY HEAD UP out of the boat. Lila was headed over for our free-diving lesson.

At first she was a little jerky, throttling too much and knocking herself backward onto the engine. Then, of course, she released the throttle and the little boat lurched to a putter and she had to brace herself on the tube in front of her.

It was mid-afternoon and hot as blazes. I'd already been in the water twice to cool off, and the coconut I'd found on my deck was long gone.

Lila waved at me. "Hi, Mia!" Her tender bumped into *Welina*'s hull and bounced off. Lila leaped up, trying to catch the toe rail of my boat, but she was too late. Bouncing off the hull had knocked the boat out of reach, and she scrambled for a minute, trying to grab it. The kill cord on her other wrist popped off the switch and the engine died.

"Oh, fuck a duck," Lila cursed. "Sorry, it's my first time driving the dinghy by myself!" she shouted as she drifted away.

"That's okay!" I called back to her. I watched her pull the starter four or five times. On the last pull, she finally got the cord out far enough that the engine kicked to life.

"Get your painter ready and you can hand it to me when you bump into *Welina*."

"Okay." Lila bundled the line tied to the bow in one hand. The other hand worked the throttle again, and she approached the side of my boat. This time, I was there to catch the line, so even though she played bumper boats, I held on so she wouldn't bump away again.

She killed the engine and stood up in the dinghy. "Victory!" She raised her fists and turned around to look at *Eik*. Eivind stood out on the bow, watching, and returned her exuberance.

She had a huge grin on her face when she turned around. "Okay, now I have to do that fifty million more times till I get it right."

"Good job," I said, thinking about when I taught Liam how to drive our dinghy and how frustrating it was. "I bet you can get it in ten."

Lila climbed aboard as I tied the line to one of *Welina*'s cleats. She fiddled with the kill cord on her wrist. "This is a bit of a pain, isn't it?"

I looked up at her. "Put it around your ankle. It should be able to stretch that far when you are driving, and then you have both hands free."

She took the cord off her wrist and lifted a foot, slipping it over and up to her ankle. "Brilliant."

I nodded toward the back and Lila made her way to the cockpit. "What's life like on *Eik* today?"

"Marcella is baking bread, Elayna's in a mood,

and the boys are going to do some boat project. Pickling the thruster? Or polishing the halyard? I don't know. Something that I don't want to get involved in. Or, actually, I don't think they want me involved in. Nor is there room."

"Yeah, a lot of boat spaces you have to squeeze into for projects are pretty small."

"Exactly. Anyway, it's hot out, and I thought now would be the perfect time to cool off with a swim."

"That sounds pretty good actually. Give me fifteen minutes to get ready?"

"I have all the stuff I need. At least I think I do. I'll wait here?"

"Sure."

I changed quickly and stepped back into the cockpit to slather on sunscreen. I opened up one of the lockers and pulled out my gear: weight belts, fins, snorkel, and mask.

"Where do you want to go snorkeling?" I asked her.

"Wherever you think would be good. You know the area better than I do."

"Let's take the dinghy over to the coral head on the other side of *Eik* and start there. It's a big coral head and the area around it is shallow, so it'll be good for breathing practice."

Lila hopped in first and I handed her my gear. "Do you want to drive?" she asked me, hopeful.

"Nah, it's all you."

She groaned. "I was afraid you would say that."

"The more you practice, the better you'll be."

I hung on to *Welina* while Lila started the engine. It took her a few tries again, and she grunted in frustration. "Any tips you want to share with me?"

I grinned at her. "You have to be really committed. Yank that fluffernutter as hard as you can."

She laughed. "Fluffernutter." She cast a spiteful look at the motor.

I opened up the little locker in the bow and pulled out the anchor. Lila and I navigated toward the coral as if there were an invisible obstacle course in the way, weaving from side to side as she steered and overcorrected.

Lila flushed, embarrassed.

"Don't worry about it," I told her. "I can't tell you how many people I've taught to drive boats and they have trouble learning how to steer too."

"Really?"

"Yeah. Even some professional captains overcorrect from time to time. It's no big deal here, especially because there's no one to run into." I gestured out at the wide and empty lagoon.

With my guidance, we dropped the anchor in the

sand and put our gear on. "Okay, lessons first, or fun first?"

"Lessons."

"Cool. So, what have you done in terms of snorkeling and free diving?"

Lila told me about practicing in a pool with Eivind and snorkeling a few times in the last anchorage. She interrupted herself. "What are you doing?"

I looked up from my mask, where I cleaned the lens. "Oh, this? It's baby shampoo. It keeps the mask from fogging up. Want to try some?"

"Yeah!" She wrinkled her nose. "Eivind and Jonas spit into their masks. It's kinda gross."

"Yeah, a lot of people do that. I've never liked it and find the baby shampoo to be better anyway." I showed her how to wash and rinse the mask out and then we put the masks on our faces. I slipped my fins on and strapped the weight belt around my waist. "I brought you a weight belt too. Since it's shallow here, we'll use these to keep ourselves closer to the bottom. You'll still float," I assured her. "But you don't have to work as hard to stay down."

I showed her how to put the belt on so that the weight sat comfortably and how to quickly release the strap and drop the weight. "Don't worry even a tiny bit about having to drop the weight. It's so shallow here, I can easily retrieve it, so if you panic or anything, pop it loose and surface. Okay?"

"Okay." We ditched our snorkels—we didn't need them.

I held my mask to my face—Lila watched and copied me—and we flipped backward out of the dinghy. I swam around to her side and she grinned at me.

"It feels weird. Not as floaty."

"True. We're going to hang on so you don't have to work so hard to stay at the surface." We both gripped the handles and stopped kicking as much. "Make sure you don't come up directly under the dinghy."

I gave Lila instructions on how to breathe at the surface and how to pop her ears if she needed to. We did some easy exercises, sinking to the bottom and staying down as long as she could.

In between dives, we rested at the surface, hanging on and chatting.

"You are pretty good at this," Lila commented.

"Thanks. I enjoy free diving, and I've practiced a lot. You'll get a lot better with more practice."

"No, I meant the teaching thing. You're a good instructor."

"Oh," I said, surprised. "Thanks."

"Did you ever teach sailing?"

"A long time ago, at summer camp when I was a counselor. It's been awhile. I mean, I guess I kind of taught Liam, but that was hard."

She grinned at me. "Some guys are pretty stubborn. Eivind and Jonas have been teaching me sailing since I joined the boat, but it's not always easy, and I think it's because they are guys."

I hummed. "Sometimes I do get frustrated because I'm not strong enough to do the things I need to. I feel that I have to be more creative to get the same results. Does that make sense?"

"Yes! And you've only got two hands too. That's another disadvantage."

"True," I agreed. I looked over at Lila. "Ready to go again?"

She nodded. We let go and dropped to the bottom.

When Lila got too tired to keep diving, we exchanged our weight belts for the snorkels and took off for the reef. We lazily kicked our way around the coral heads, looking at the colorful fish and other wildlife that lived underwater.

I made sure to point out things to Lila that I thought were interesting; she squealed when I showed her the Christmas tree worms, with their two brightly colored tree-shaped antennae waving around and catching food. When I swept my hand in front of them, they sucked their antennae in and hid. We saw them in so many colors: red, pink, blue, purple, and yellow.

Lila yelped when I pointed out a shark, a small black-tipped reef shark lazily swimming around. He gave us a wide berth and swam off into the distance behind us.

We snorkeled till my butt felt toasty from too much sun, but I was loath to leave. Having a friend to experience the reef with was so much more fun, and seeing everything through Lila's eyes was invigorating, reminding me that this cruising life was worth doing.

SIX

Back on the boat, I offered Lila a freshwater shower and a drink. She had pulled herself up into the dinghy laughing and giddy from the snorkeling, and her mood was infectious.

We both rinsed off and I changed clothes while Lila stretched out on the bow to sunbathe herself dry.

"What do you want to drink?" I called out the open hatch.

"Gin and tonic?"

"Ah, well, I don't have any ice. Or cold tonic water. Or gin."

Lila's head poked through the hatch and she looked at me. "What *do* you have?"

"Sorry, I'm not much of the drunken sailor type." I counted off my fingers. "Beer. Beer. Maybe some box wine? And for sure, I definitely have a thing of beer."

She grinned. "Beer it is."

I slipped two cold beers into koozies and brought them to the cockpit, where Lila met me. "Is it okay to sit on the cushions, even though I'm all wet?"

"Go for it." She flopped against the backrest and stretched her legs out.

"Cheers for the beer." She tipped the can to her lips and took a swig.

"How are you liking cruising?" I asked her.

She smiled at me. "Well, if you don't count the passage across the Pacific, it has been great."

I laughed. "So I guess you'd like the sailing lifestyle better without the sailing bits, huh?"

She threw her head back against the cushions. "It was *so long*. And there was a buildup of things and tensions, and at the end you feel all confused and tangled up." She gestured wildly with her hand.

"I know the feeling. I like sailing, but even I was glad to have that passage be done with."

"You're like Jonas. He likes sailing too. Like, the skill of it and technical stuff. Not to say that he doesn't enjoy the island hopping, but . . ."

I nodded. "Yeah, that's how I feel. I like to be out at sea. It's calming."

"Sure, when everything goes well and you know you'll see land in a day or two."

"Okay, so you like the island hopping best. Got it." I smiled at her. "Tell me about your time in the Marquesas."

She ticked off the islands. "Fatu Hiva, Hiva Oa, Tahuatu, Nuku Hiva . . ." She told me about searching for tikis and grating coconut and eating *poisson cru* at the cafés.

We talked about each island, her with the joy of new discoveries and me with nostalgia. "Did you . . . ?" and "We loved . . ." and "I want to go back."

"It's really interesting how the Marquesas Islands are so different from the Tuamotus."

"Yeah, it was like a jungle out there. Here is more like a tropical paradise."

We sipped our drinks and stared out at the blue water around us.

Lila changed the topic. "Okay, it was so weird to see Jonas last night. He was so nervous! It was like he'd forgotten how to be a normal socializing adult."

I giggled, my cheeks pinking. "Aw, I know. I feel bad for him and I don't know how to make him more comfortable. He definitely has his sweet moments, but . . ."

She nodded firmly. "Even Eivind teased him last night after he got back from taking you home. I told

Eivind to butt out, that he was only making it worse." She turned to face me. "Did you know he's divorced too?"

"No, I didn't."

"Nah, yeah. A few years ago. He doesn't talk about it much, but I gather that it's part of the reason why the boys took off sailing."

"Divorce is tough." I stared off into the distance and picked at my koozie.

"What happened between you and your husband? If you don't mind me asking."

"It's fine," I said, brushing her concern away. "Cruising, or even just sailing, can make or break a couple, and it broke us. Things were already bad before we left Mexico, but they got worse quickly."

Lila shivered. "You make it sound so ominous." She chewed on her lip and gazed out at *Eik*. "That makes me worry sometimes. Like, I haven't known Eivind all that long, so what if that happens to us?"

"I don't think the length of time you know someone has anything to do with it. I knew Liam for years. We weren't close, but we had mutual friends our first few semesters in college and hung out together at the same parties. Then we dated for a year, got engaged, married a little while later." I shook my head. "You think you know someone so well, but even after years, you can learn new things.

Or they can change." The wrinkles of concern on Lila's brow had smoothed out a little bit. "You and Eivind have been through a lot together already. Crossing the Pacific is no small feat."

She gave me a small smile in sympathy and then cocked her head. "Do you regret going cruising?"

I smiled weakly. "Well, I wouldn't be here. I think it was good we did. Maybe you need to bring out the worst in people sometimes."

Lila winced and looked at me carefully. "That sounds painful."

I didn't really want to talk about how my marriage had deteriorated. While I didn't regret cruising, I wondered what the experience would be like with a partner who was gentler, kinder, and who looked out for me. I changed the subject.

"How about Marcella and Elayna? Do they like cruising?"

"Well, Marcella is going to leave us soon—she's had enough of the sailing aspect. She'd rather be in the galley cooking up fancy meals. Elayna loves it, but she's a bit of a party girl. I think she wouldn't even be on the boat any longer if she hadn't . . ." Lila hesitated. "Well, if she hadn't had a thing for Jonas."

"I can understand that. They are both attractive."

"Yeah. I think sometimes it's inevitable with these remote islands and lack of a social scene that crew members can become bedfellows. I mean, look what happened with Eivind and me after all. And, well"—she leaned in conspiratorially—"Jonas and Elayna do have some history."

"Oh?"

"Apparently, Elayna had a crush on Jonas, and for a while, they were not a couple exactly, but hooking up. It came to a head after the Panama Canal. Jonas just doesn't feel that way about her, and Elayna was a little crushed."

"I thought there was some tension between them."

There must have been something in the way I said it because Lila hastily clarified, "It's not like that really. Jonas just wasn't interested in her like that, and Elayna accepted it but is still getting over it, and perhaps she's a little upset with herself for getting into this situation. With you around and Jonas so obviously fangirling over you . . ." She rolled her eyes. "I'm feeling really gossipy right now. Sorry."

"I would imagine it's hard to have five people in a small space and not a lot of options for socializing. And also, no internet."

"Nah, yeah. My mum's not thrilled that she doesn't hear from me regularly. It's like being out at sea in that respect." She thinks for a moment. "Actually, I kind of like that."

"It is nice to disconnect. But, yeah, my family hates it too."

"You know what's worse? Having slow and shitty internet. Like, I would much rather have no internet over slow internet."

"I know! Me too! Nothing is more frustrating than a web page taking forever to load."

We both giggled. "Jonas does some work remotely, scientific writing or editing or something like that. Even with everything that we've been through together, I've never seen him as pissed off as in the Marquesas when you could get 'internet'"— she air-quoted it—"but really it was a complete waste. He could hardly download new assignments."

"Oh, that's tough, especially if you have remote work to do. French Polynesia isn't really the place for it."

"I think or, I guess, I hope, that it'll be better in Tahiti so he can get some work done."

"I could use some internet myself too. It's been a while."

"Jonas says there's a Wi-Fi café in Fakarava." Fakarava was the next island over, a place I'd considered for my next stop.

A sharp whistle blew from *Eik*, and we turned to find Eivind waving his arms at us.

"Whoops, I guess it's almost dinnertime. I gotta go. Thanks for the beer, and the girl talk."

"Anytime."

I helped Lila take off and watched her dinghy across to *Eik*. The sunset was in its full glory, the ocean reflecting the sky like molten gold, disturbed only by the ripples of her wake.

SEVEN

A KNOCK SOUNDED ON MY HULL WHILE I WAS MAKING breakfast. "Come on in!" I yelled out the companionway.

I heard the various noises of someone climbing onto the boat. I was freshly cleaned, having swum that morning in the cool, crisp water around my boat. I had watched Jonas paddle to shore and wander around in the dawn; an early riser, he was.

He appeared in my companionway, carrying a coconut in one hand. I smiled at him, and he reached down to pass it to me, our fingers brushing.

I laughed. "Thank you for the coconuts. I love them."

He smiled shyly. "They are your favorite."

I gently wedged the coconut in my freezer to chill

faster. It would be perfectly cool in the afternoon heat. "Where are you getting them from?"

He gestured vaguely toward shore and leaned against the counter opposite me. "Onshore there are husking sticks set up. Have you not seen them?"

Shaking my head, I answered, "I've seen the husking shack, but not husking sticks. I don't even know what they look like or how to use one." An idea popped into my head. I finished slathering peanut butter onto my toast and took a bite, eyeing Jonas. My galley was so small, I had to stand diagonal to Jonas so there was room for his feet. I lifted my foot and poked his calf with my toe. "Is it hard?"

"Husking coconuts?" I nodded. "If you have the right tools, it is not so bad."

I swallowed a bite. "Can you show me how to do it?"

His face changed, surprised to delighted. "It takes some time to get used to. If you know the right technique, it is much easier."

"Where did you learn?"

"In Hiva Oa. We rented a car from a local and drove around the island. Everyone was so friendly and generous. When we returned the car, the trunk was full of fruit. We had nearly a dozen coconuts and no idea what to do with them. The owner offered to show us how to husk the coconuts and make the milk, so we did."

"That is a good skill to have as a cruiser."

"Ja. But now that I know how to do it, Marcella insists on only cooking with fresh coconut milk. It is a lot of husking," he said with a smile. His shoulders relaxed, his body loosening.

I took the last bite of my toast and dusted my hands off. "Maybe I don't want you to teach me. Then I'll have to get my own coconuts every day."

Jonas laughed and pushed off the counter, heading back up the stairs. "I will go get the other paddleboard and come get you."

"Okay."

I followed him out onto the deck, and while he climbed onto his paddleboard, I grabbed my clothes from yesterday off the lifeline. The pieces were dry and clean enough after a freshwater rinse.

By the time I'd changed and applied sunscreen, Jonas was back.

As I sat on the toe rail of *Welina*, Jonas paddled closer to me before dropping to his knees on his board.

I gripped the stanchions on either side as Jonas maneuvered my paddleboard to the inside and he crowded it into the right position. I stretched my legs down, but I could barely brush the top of the board with the tip of my toe.

"Can you reach?" His forehead wrinkled in concern.

I weighed my options. It was just a bit too far for me to make it, and *Welina* didn't have a stern platform like *Eik* did.

"Hm. Let me try something else." Odds were pretty good that I would be falling off my paddleboard at some point today—I might as well get it over with. I stood up and walked down the deck until I cleared the two paddleboards. Gripping the shroud, I swung my legs over the lifelines, looked down, and dove.

As warm as it was, the water still held a bit of bite in the early morning. I surfaced and shook the water off my face. Jonas had drifted away from *Welina* with both paddleboards and now he grinned at me.

I took a few strokes to swim over to my board and grip the edge. There was a handle in the center of the board that gave me a perfect holding point. I got halfway up, resting my forearms and chest on the board. "Huh. This is actually pretty stable." When Jonas didn't answer, I glanced up.

Jonas looked away quickly and stammered. "Uh, yes, stable . . ."

Did I have a booger? I swiped at my nose and tried to discreetly wriggle anything out. Hm. Nothing. Why were we back to nervous, shy Jonas again?

I caught his eyes flashing at me once more, and looked down. Oh fudgepuckers. One boob had popped out of my bathing suit top, my nipple peeking out over the material.

I slid back down into the water and readjusted my bikini top to properly cover myself. I should have known better than to dive off the deck, but I'd gotten so used to wearing rash guards for the sun protection.

"Okay, let's try that again." I hauled myself up, but this time I kept going and swung my legs up to get fully on the board. I sat up on my knees and checked the girls again. All good.

"I'm up and I'm presentable. Jonas, you can look now."

He turned back to me, his face flushed.

"No, bring back Jonas! I made it weird now," I teased.

Jonas gave me a small smile and cleared his throat. He reached over and tapped my leg. "Give me your ankle." I straightened one leg and he attached the leash of my board to my ankle. He handed me the paddle and my snorkel gear, which I tucked under the bungee on the nose of the board. Jonas then showed me how to stand up, balance myself, and paddle around.

I steadied myself on the board and we set off for the shore.

It was a slow, easy paddle to the motu, and I stepped off into the shallows as my board hit the sand. The inflatable paddleboards were light enough that I could tuck mine under my arm and carry it farther up to drier sand, where it wouldn't get washed away. We dumped our paddles in the sand and I looked at Jonas.

"First, we need a coconut." He took off along the beach. The motu was narrow, a small strip of land protecting the lagoon from the ocean. In one direction was a clearing in the trees, where I knew the copra shack was, and a break in the land where the water flowed between motus. We went the other way, where there was more land to explore.

Jonas and I walked side by side. The sand was white and soft, the waves of the lagoon barely a few inches tall, and we shaded our eyes, peering up into the trees to look for coconuts. "Do those work?" I pointed out a tree with three heavy green globes hanging down.

He made a noise in the back of his throat. "Those

are okay, but this one . . ." He pointed off to the side. "This one is better." The tree he walked toward leaned way over, the trunk running along the beach before swooping toward the sun. That was a better choice; it'd be easier to reach the coconuts.

When we stood under the coconuts, they were further up than I'd thought. Even on his tippy-toes, it was a stretch for Jonas to reach them. But he managed, using a pocketknife to cut the stem. He shook the coconut, and we heard the water sloshing around inside the nut. Jonas tossed it down into the sand, and picked three more.

I scooped a coconut under each arm. "Hmm," I said. "I think our eyes are bigger than our arms. We can't carry any more."

We walked back, past our paddleboards to the husking station. It was a reminder of traditional times, when copra, the fibrous husks of coconuts, used to be the main industry in the islands. Copra was still harvested, dried, and sold in many of the South Pacific islands, but as the population of the villages dwindled due to better opportunities elsewhere, the small islands like Kauehi didn't produce copra like they used to anymore.

"This is the husking stick." Jonas stood beside a dark rod sticking out of the sand. If I didn't know to look for it, I could have easily mistaken it for a slight tree branch. When I looked closer, I saw that the rod was made of metal, the end sticking up sharp and pointed.

Jonas dropped the coconuts by his feet. "Are you ready for your lesson now?" I dropped one of the coconuts from my arms, and it thunked as it hit the ground. The other one I handed to him and he inspected it carefully.

With both hands he held it, bringing it over his head and then down sharply onto the stick. The husk split, the rod embedded in the coconut. Jonas adjusted his fingers, using the crack in the husk to grip and twist. A large chunk of the husk came off and fell to the ground.

He repeated the move two more times until there was only a small strip of husk left, which he grasped with his bare hands and ripped from the nut.

And then all that was left was the husked nut, ready to whack open and drink.

"You make it look so easy."

"It is not so bad. Finding a good coconut is harder."

"Okay, my turn." I picked up a coconut and hip-checked Jonas out of the way. I raised it above my head and eyeballed the stake. "Jesus." Then I did a stupid thing: I closed my eyes and attempted to impale the coconut on the stake.

Thank God, I managed to hit the stake, but instead of piercing the husk, the coconut bounced off and out of my hands and thudded into the sand. Jonas burst out laughing, bending in half and gripping his stomach.

"Hey now," I protested. "Not bad for the first time."

He was still chuckling when he cocked his head at me. "Not bad?"

I held up my hand and wiggled my fingers. "I still have ten fingers. And thank God we weren't filming."

Jonas smiled at me, wide and bright. He picked up the coconut and handed it to me. "This time, eyes on your coconut." He tapped my temple. "Keep them open." He helped me slide my hands around to keep them out of the way. I tried again, this time with a better grip, and I impaled it on the stake with a solid thunk.

I pressed the coconut onto the stake with my body, jiggling it, leaning all my weight onto it and trying to separate the husk, and suddenly it gave.

Twisting was hard; the outer shell was slippery in my hands and I couldn't quite get a grip on the crack like Jonas did. I wrestled with it for a little bit while Jonas watched, but I finally got it. The rest of the husk came off more easily and we had two husked coconuts.

I wiped the sweat off my brow. "Easier than some of the more creative ways I've tried to get one open."

Jonas smiled and offered me another coconut. I did it, but my hands were getting tired and I let him husk coconut number four.

"So," I said slyly. "How many of these are for me?"

Jonas threw his head back and laughed, Adam's apple bobbing. "How many do you want?"

"Well, at least one." He nodded. "I know you have quite a few people on board who might like a coconut."

He waggled his head back and forth. "I do not think any of them will get the enjoyment out of it that you do. Maybe Lila."

"How about a compromise? You take one back to Lila and leave me three."

"That does not sound fair. After all my work today, picking a coconut and husking it for you, I do not get one?"

I smirked at him. "Negotiate with me."

"One for Lila, one for me, and two for you."

"One for Eivind to give to Lila, three for me, but I'll let you drink one of mine on my boat this afternoon."

"Only if it's cold."

"Deal."

Jonas shook his head, laughing. "But now we have to paddle all four of the coconuts back."

"Oh God."

EIGHT

JONAS AND I GOT THE PADDLEBOARDS BACK IN THE water and let the coconuts bob next to us while we climbed on. It was like a Three Stooges show: Jonas balanced two coconuts on his board, two on mine, but when he tried to get on his board, one rolled off. I helped him get the coconut back and both of mine rolled backward off the board.

We were both laughing so hard that Jonas fell in, and I had to drop to my knees and paddle around, rescuing his wards.

Finally I wedged three coconuts between my shins and stayed on my knees, paddling back to *Welina*. Jonas waved and headed toward *Eik*, and I knew I'd see him soon for cold coconuts.

It was later in the afternoon than I expected it to be when I heard *Eik*'s dinghy sputter to life. Instead of coming to my boat, though, the dinghy was full of the entire crew and they motored to shore.

I frowned, strangely disappointed that I had two coconuts to enjoy all by myself, when I noticed the dinghy pulling back from shore and turning toward my boat. Jonas picked up speed, zooming in a wide circle around *Welina* before cutting the engine and drifting over to my side.

"Mia," he called out, grabbing the edge of my boat. "Grab the coconuts and come to the beach."

Jonas waited while I gathered up some things to take with me: a beach towel, bug spray, my camera. When I was ready, I stepped down into the dinghy and Jonas shot us toward the shore.

He threw an anchor out and the tender drifted in, bumping the beach. I climbed out and Jonas handed me my bags.

"Mia!" Lila called out to me. "We're having a barbie!"

"I can see that."

"Eivind and Jonas went spearfishing this afternoon," Marcella told me. She wrapped some large reef fish in aluminum foil while Jonas joined Eivind to help him build a fire. Elayna poked in the trees, picking up wood. "We will have reef fish curry tonight."

"Yum," I said. "I was going to set my camera up if that's okay with everyone?" I asked the general group. They all nodded. "Then can I help?"

Marcella gestured to a bag. "There are blankets in there, and a cooler with drinks. You can set up a place to sit."

I set up my camera first, getting the tripod together and adjusting the settings to be just right: a little overexposed to carry us through the sunset. After initiating the time-lapse feature, I stepped back and around to the fire.

I worked spreading out the blankets and my own beach towel around where the guys were piling sticks and coconut husks. They had a small bottle of gasoline to get it lit, and it ignited with a loud *whoosh*.

Jonas turned to find me and wiped his hands off on his shorts. "You brought the coconuts?" he asked hopefully.

"I did." I grabbed the bag that contained the two coconuts, a large sheathed knife, and two reusable straws.

I palmed one of the coconuts out of the bag and held it up. "This one must be mine; it's looking a little ragged."

"Do you need help?"

"Nah, I got this part. The husking is the hard part." With one hand, I pulled the knife out and pushed the sheath off with my thumb. I found the three soft spots and pointed them upward. Angling the knife slightly downward, I chopped into the shell right below the eyes.

Like a basketball, I rotated it ninety degrees and chopped into it again. Turn, chop, turn, chop. I cut a small square into the top, which I pried out with my fingers. Bending down, I plucked out a straw and popped it into the water.

"Ta-da!"

I looked up to find the entire crew watching me, and Lila enthusiastically applauded. I offered it to Jonas, who took it in his hands and sipped through the straw. He smacked his lips with a sigh. "Still cold."

I repeated the process with mine and sat cross-legged on my towel, resting the coconut in my lap. Jonas wedged his into the space by the edge of the blanket and threw some more logs onto the fire, building it up. It tilted into evening now, the sun creeping toward the horizon and the shadows getting longer.

Jonas sat down next to me, wriggling his butt into the sand to get comfortable. Even with the slight heat from the fire in front of me, I could feel the warmth radiating from him. I snuck looks at him out of the corner of my eye. We faced the sunset together and the warm pinks and reds reflected in his eyes and made his hair, loose again now, glow.

Lila and Elayna were laughing about something, but I couldn't take my eyes off Jonas.

He glanced over at me, his smile slipping as his expression became more serious. We watched each other for a moment until Jonas cleared his throat and broke our eye contact. I swallowed and looked down at my coconut, fiddling with the coarse husk.

Jonas's chin tilted back behind us at my camera, set up on the tripod. "That is filming now?"

"Yup." I leaned back on my towel and watched as Marcella carefully placed the packets of fish in the flames and sat back on her heels. Jonas paused for a moment, poking the fire and watching the flames. He glanced behind us at my camera again.

"Jonas, stop!" I laughed. "Stop looking at the camera. Just act natural, or I'll turn it off."

He turned back reluctantly. "I do not know how you do it. How do you ignore the camera?"

"Practice," I said.

Elayna crouched down and dusted some sand off the blanket on the other side of Jonas. "What are you doing with this video anyway? I thought you were not filming."

I took a sip from my coconut while Elayna sat down. "I don't have any plans for it, but even if it doesn't get published, at least tonight is memorialized somewhere, right?"

"What is that expression?" she asked. "Pictures or it's not real?"

"Something like that," I muttered.

Elayna tossed her hair. "One of the things I like about sailing out here is that we can disconnect, live in the moment, yes? Well, except for our relationships." She looped her arm around Marcella. "I wouldn't trade my time with this crew for anything."

I looked away into the fire as the crew of *Eik* had a moment together, everyone happy and me the interloper.

Jonas leaned forward, his knee bending to brush against mine, and poked the fire with his stick. "I think we might need some more coconut husks."

Lila jumped up and dusted her shorts off. "We should get more before it gets too dark. Elayna, help me?" She beamed a smile and held out her hand to Elayna.

While the girls wandered around the tree line, Eivind shifted over to sit next to Jonas.

The sunlight faded, and we talked as the fire grew brighter and the sky dimmed. Sunset curled its arms out, the clouds massive colorful tentacles in the sky.

Marcella had pulled the fish out, and once they had cooled enough, she picked the meat off the bones and mixed it into a large pot with rice and curry.

My coconut was empty, so I put it in my bag to scoop out the insides later. Jonas did the same, and Elayna and Marcella worked together dishing out dinner. I stretched my legs out and thanked Elayna for the bowl.

We ate by firelight, the stars fully out above us. Jonas was warm next to me, and when he shifted on the towel, the sand underneath shifted too, and it pulled me closer to him.

The other women sat across the fire from me. Eivind was at his brother's side, and they talked about something in Norwegian. I lay back on the towel, letting my eyes adjust to the sky instead of the fire, and stargazed.

Eventually Marcella, Elayna, and Lila set off along the beach for a walk, the moon and stars lighting their way. Eivind stirred the fire and then went to hunt for more firewood in the trees.

With a little grunt, Jonas leaned back to rest beside me.

"Thank you for coming tonight."

"Thank you for the invitation." I stretched my arms out over my head and smiled at the moon before I turned to look at Jonas. I thought he'd looked good in the firelight and the fading dusk, but the night sky gave him a sharper edge. "I don't really get to do these kinds of things anymore. It's less fun when you are by yourself."

"Hmmm. What did you do last time you were here?"

"Oh . . ." I took a deep breath. "Liam and I had a fight. We were having trouble with the watermaker, and we were still reeling from the Pacific crossing. I was . . . I was just starting to really consider leaving him." My throat closed up, the words getting caught there. Jonas shifted in the sand next to me, a tug on my back—or maybe my soul—pulling me toward him. Then his palm slid down my forearm, his fingers twining with mine.

"This place deserves good memories instead."

NINE

THE KNOCKING ON THE HULL WAS NOT GOING AWAY. I already knew who it was: Jonas. He was always up before anyone else in the mornings.

Then the knock had an accompaniment. "Mia. Mia! Get out of bed."

I climbed into the cockpit and shaded my eyes. Jonas's face was over the toe rail, which he held in one hand while gripping a paddle with the other.

"A little bird told me you would like to go paddleboarding." His voice was more confident and comfortable, and I could almost forget that he was a superfan.

"It's early," I whined, rubbing my eyes. "Can we go later?"

Jonas pointed up, and I tipped my head back. The sky was molting toward blue, but the sunrise still dominated and it was absolutely cloudless. "It is going to be very still today. And very hot later." Jonas looked back at me. "Come on."

Leaning over the edge of the cockpit, I noticed the second paddleboard bobbing in the water next to Jonas. He could see me relenting and a smile erupted from his face. He released the side of my boat to grab the paddle in both hands and hold it over his head in triumph. "Victory!"

A startled laugh burst out of me and he grinned. "Go." He waved me away. "I will wait. Bring a snorkel and a mask."

Jonas let his paddleboard drift while I ducked back inside to change. I put on a rash guard and bikini bottom and slathered some sunscreen on my exposed skin. I chugged a glass of water before grabbing my snorkel gear and swinging my legs over the side of the cockpit.

Just like last time, I dove off the side of *Welina* into the glassy water. This time, my boobs were properly covered by the rash guard.

Once I was standing up and stable on my board, I looked over my shoulder at Jonas.

"Very good." He nodded toward the beach. "Now we will head to the shore and take a left and follow along the beach for as long as we want."

Distance and effort made it hard to carry on a

conversation, and I was too busy focusing on my paddling. Occasionally, Jonas gave me tips.

We hopped from coral head to coral head, peering down from our standing position into the glassy waters below. With no wind, we didn't have to worry about being blown too far, and the shore was always within easy reach. I looked back to find the boats nearly two miles from us.

The sun and lack of breeze had taken its toll. Sweat dripped down my forehead, collecting under my breasts and at my lower back. Jonas must have been feeling the same, even though he paddled in only swim trunks. He dropped to his knees and swapped the paddle for the snorkel gear under the bungee.

"Time to cool off!" Jonas's teeth flashed at me before he put the snorkel in his mouth and launched himself off the board and into the water.

As I dropped down to my butt, throwing my legs into the water on either side of the paddleboard, I watched Jonas swim beneath the surface. His paddleboard gave a jerk when he reached the end of the leash, and then dutifully followed him from above. Jonas popped up next to my right knee, clearing his snorkel and treading water.

As the water slid up my calves, it chilled me, and

I groaned. I quickly put my mask and snorkel on and rolled over the side of the board.

There was nothing quite as enjoyable as slipping into the cool waters of the Pacific on a hot day. Without air conditioning, boats tended to get hot and stuffy. Add in slaving away on a boat project, and there had been many days when I'd been a frustrated, sticky mess. But a dip off the boat never ceased to wash it all away.

Jonas and I swam back in the direction of the boats. Without our fins, we weren't moving terribly quickly or diving down below the surface. We watched clown fish dart in and out of their homes and black-tipped reef sharks swim past without even acknowledging our presence.

Eventually we hauled ourselves onto the boards again. Jonas lay on his back, one leg dangling in the water, the other propped up on my board, keeping us floating together. His hands were clasped behind his head, his eyes closed. With both of my legs in the water, I sat up, leaning back on my hands.

"Thank you," I said. Jonas lifted his head to look at me, squinting in the sun. He smiled and patted my knee. I shimmied myself down toward the nose of the board so I could lie down too. I raised my leg underneath Jonas's and rested my heel on his board. My thigh, heated from the warm sun, pressed against the back of his ankle. I let my other foot dangle in the water, keeping me cool.

"I always wanted a paddleboard. We almost got some as a sponsorship. We were supposed to fly back to the boat with them."

"They are pretty great. Easy to use, and they store well. I like . . ." Jonas hesitated and turned toward me. Our heads had drifted apart, so he reached out and pulled me closer with his fingertips. I wound my arm under his, linking our elbows together to keep us from drifting apart. "I like the solitude it gives me. With five of us on board, the boat is always a place of action. Someone wants to play music or is working on projects or whatever. Even the sounds of the boat or the dinghy can be grating to me sometimes. But the paddleboard, it is so peaceful and freeing."

"Yes, I think so too." We drifted in silence for a few moments. "I wish we'd gotten a paddleboard anyway. I can't get the dinghy down by myself; it's too hard."

"A paddleboard would be great for a solo sailor. Easier to handle by yourself."

"Right." I closed my eyes, feeling the heat of the sun baking my skin. My foot spun in lazy circles under the surface of the water.

"What made you decide to go cruising?" I asked Jonas.

"You did." He answered so quickly and confidently, it took me a moment to process his words.

"Me?" I turned my head to look at him.

"Ja, you, and the other sailing channels out there." He laughed to himself. "I was, like . . ." He searched for the words in the clouds above us. "Maybe having a breakdown?" He looked at me with a little grin and I couldn't help but laugh, even though it wasn't really funny.

"A breakdown? Like mentally?"

"Ja." He nodded.

"I cannot see that at all."

"It was a very manly breakdown," he teased. "I called Eivind and told him to come by, and I was overly excited and maybe I had not showered in a few days and the place was a mess. But I sat him down and showed him the videos, all these sailors out doing amazing things. Your videos, especially when you were in Mexico." He grinned sheepishly. "I may not have shown him the boatyard videos."

"Good call. And Eivind just agreed to go with you?"

"You should ask him about it sometime. He looked at me and the videos and the mess in my place and said, 'Okay.'"

"Wow."

Jonas looked off into the distance, and I watched

the smile on his lips fade. "I wish," he started, "that I'd had someone else to ask. It makes me feel lonely."

"Even with the right person to ask, it can still be lonely."

Jonas turned to look at me and I dropped my eyes, embarrassed that I'd shared something so deeply personal.

"Do you like cruising?" Jonas asked.

"Of course I do. It's such a great lifestyle." I cringed at how rote my words sounded; I hoped he wouldn't notice the hollowness.

He grunted beside me. "It's different than I thought it would be."

"How so?"

He thought for a moment. "When I started watching videos, like yours, online, I thought, yes, this is what I want. My wife would have never agreed to do this. But I can see that doing it with a partner is easier in a lot of ways. Having my brother with me, and the additional crew members, it is more responsibility than I thought it would be. There is too much . . . complexity?"

"I would imagine so." I thought about this for a moment. "I guess you have to be responsible for them, and work out shift logistics and money, stuff like that."

"Yes." He nodded. "It is complex. And when Lila

came on board to be with Eivind, perhaps I see now that they enjoy it more because they are together."

"That's good, right?"

"It is good for Eivind," he said. "But it makes my heart ache a little for what might have been."

He fell silent and I thought back on my time sailing with Liam and the ups and downs of our relationship.

"Sailing with a partner is hard too, though."

"Yes, I am certain that is true." He turned his head to look at me expectantly.

"Maybe it's like having a kid. Sometimes it makes you stronger and sometimes it makes you weaker. If there are cracks, they start to show. And the cracks grow so quickly."

"Ja."

And with that depressing thought, we lapsed into silence, drifting lazily, two divorced people bumping together out in the big world.

———

I watched Lila paddle toward me in the late afternoon. She had been practicing most days, while Jonas and I had gotten into a routine of paddling together the past few mornings.

Lila steered the board around to *Welina*'s stern,

where she grabbed the rail and grinned at me. "What do you say to some happy hour?" She gestured to a bag at her feet. "I even came with supplies."

"Sounds great. Do you want to come in out of the sun?" It was still pretty hot out, and though we had a slight breeze, we were going to be sweaty no matter where we sat.

"Actually"—Lila lifted her sunglasses up—"I was thinking we could open a swim-up bar right here." She carefully bent down and detached the tether from her ankle and secured it to *Welina*'s railing. Tucking the paddle up on *Welina*'s deck, Lila slid off the board and rested her elbows on the top of the paddleboard. She knocked on the "bar." "Oh, barkeep!"

"Oh, good idea. Let me change."

"Fine, but I'm starting without you."

When I came back out, Lila was leaning back, floating under the board with her toes sticking out of the water on the other side. I dove in and resurfaced next to her. A cold beer already waited for me and I took a sip before mirroring Lila.

She sighed in contentment. "The water feels so good."

"Mmm," I said in agreement. "It's very hot in *Welina*."

"On *Eik* too. I think some of us are getting a little

stir-crazy, and it's time to move on soon. The heat's really exacerbating things, though."

"Oh? Moving on?" I peeked at Lila.

She caught me looking, and grinned. "Jonas's plan is to get to New Zealand before cyclone season." I nodded. Most boats flew through the islands to get to safe haven before the seasons changed. "I don't think Jonas really wants to leave," she continued, raising an eyebrow at me. "I think he's having too much fun."

"I'm having fun with him. You were right: he's a different person now that he's gotten over the initial excitement."

"Yeah, I knew he just needed some time. He's pretty calm normally, so Eivind just loves being able to tease Jonas about you."

"How are things with you and Eivind? Are you the stir-crazy ones?"

"Yeah, nah. Eivind's pretty chill about wherever we go, and I certainly don't have anything to add to it. I don't know much about the navigating or timing or whatever of us getting to New Zealand. It wasn't even my plan to stay on—I'm just the hitchhiker. But Marcella needs internet to find a new position, and Elayna needs more of a social life. No one's interested in partying with her."

"What will you and Eivind do when you get to New Zealand?"

"Ah, Eivind has promised me that we will fly to Straya and he'll meet my parents. I think it's going to be hilarious. Dad likes to bust Eivind's balls. My mom, on the other hand . . . I told Eivind we can't get sucked in. We have to have an escape plan."

I laughed. "Your dad and my dad might be pretty similar. My dad likes to tease us all the time."

"Do you miss your family?"

I puffed out a breath. "Yeah, a lot. We're pretty close."

"You stayed with them when you were Stateside?"

"Yeah."

Lila paused in thought. "How long has your divorce been official?"

"Not even three months yet. I left as soon as it was done to come back to *Welina*."

Her mouth tilted down into a frown. "That's not very long. You seem to be doing pretty well, and maybe you are moving on?"

"Ah, well, I mean . . . I wouldn't say moving on."

Lila grinned slyly. "You like Jonas, right?"

I blushed. "If you are asking if I think he's attractive, then yes."

She laughed. "Okay, just making sure. I understand that the whole living situation is complicated. But you guys would make a cute couple."

"Whoa, whoa, whoa. That's not . . . We've just . . ."

Lila slipped a bit on the paddleboard and sputtered in the salty water as she giggled. "You've just what? Been spending all your time together? Are attracted to each other?"

"Yes, but . . ." I glanced over at *Eik*, and to the beach beyond, wondering how to explain myself to a bright-eyed girl in love and a decade younger than me. "It's not an easy situation. There wouldn't be much hope for a long-term relationship, and . . . I don't know. I would feel weird with anything short-term. I'm just not that kind of girl."

Lila nodded. "That's fair. To each her own, you know? I held off on doing anything with Eivind for a while, because my adventure—that experience of crossing the Panama Canal—was more important to me. But then I allowed myself to be with Eivind for a few days, then a month, and then . . ." She shrugged. "Then I fell in love. It's complicated and messy, with my wanderlust tangled up in my love for Eivind. But even if they were both temporary, I would never regret it."

My jaded heart was trapped in regret. Lila sensed my mood shift and said gently, "You should just enjoy yourself, even if it's just spending time together." She put her hand on my arm and squeezed, her lips tilted up in a smirk. "I know he loves hanging out with his favorite celebrity." She winked, and I groaned.

We continued to bob in the cool waters until Eivind called Lila home.

———

Eik HAD BEEN IN KAUEHI WITH ME FOR TWENTY DAYS. Every time I asked Jonas when they would move on, he shrugged, and a big part of me was glad. I had mulled over Lila's words, thinking about regret and love and Jonas. Every time I was with him, watching his slow smile or his strong hands, I worried I was too chicken to take any chances. Soon, *Eik* would leave. What would I regret more: Saying goodbye as friends, or taking a chance at feeling something new?

The time came, though. Jonas paddled over to tell me they were leaving in the morning.

"Where will you go next?" I asked as we sat in my cockpit together. I picked at the bench cushion, worrying the fabric between my nails, wondering how badly I would miss him, what it would feel like to look up tomorrow and not see *Eik* next to me.

"Fakarava. Have you been there?"

I shook my head. "I hear it's amazing."

Jonas leaned forward, resting his elbows on his knees and clasping his hands together. "You should come with us." He watched me, his eyes steady on mine as my heart danced in my chest.

"I don't know. I like it here." *But I'd miss you.*

"But you might like Fakarava even better," he argued, and despite his seriousness, I couldn't help the smile that grew on my face. "And you need food and internet." He pointedly looked at my pathetically empty produce hammock. "I bet your family would like to hear from you."

I chewed on my lip. "Well, that is true."

He tapped his hand against my bare knee, then gripped it, finally giving me a real smile, perhaps feeling that he'd won already. "Come with us," he said softly. "We will have fun exploring together. And I know you do not need it, but I like keeping you company."

TEN

I watched *Eik* raise its anchor and motor off toward the pass. It was a little early for the slack tide, but Jonas was watching the conditions for me and reporting back. I myself had an ulterior motive; I didn't want the crew of *Eik* to see me get the anchor up myself.

I had done it a handful of times, but it was ungainly and hard. Without *Eik* in view, I could do whatever I needed to do to get the anchor up.

Driving the boat forward, I tried to get her to hover over the anchor. I hustled to the bow and it was a complicated dance of pushing the button to haul the chain up electronically, lying on my belly to get the chain out of the way in the locker, and keeping an eye on our position.

Finally the anchor was up and secure. I quickly

went back to the helm and swung the bow out toward the pass. There was no way I could catch up to *Eik*, but Jonas did call on the VHF radio while going through: the path was clear and the current was good. I carefully threaded my way out of the pass of Kauehi.

Overnight, I'd thought about the memories I had accumulated. It was still hard not to think about my first visit with Liam and the fights that had unraveled here, but I also had new memories. Living by myself, independent for the first time since my divorce, had been hard.

But bright spots were there too. Bonfires, paddleboarding, snorkeling: thanks to my new friends, I was reminded of what this life could be like. I'd been hesitant when Jonas asked me, but now I was more confident that I was ready to move on.

Shaking myself out of my thoughts, I looked ahead to Fakarava. The winds were good, light but from a favorable direction. I rolled the jib out, telling myself I'd see how things went before going through the stress of getting the mainsail up.

As the islands of the Tuamotus were so low, I quickly lost sight of Kauehi.

As if sensing my sadness, Jonas called on the radio. "I am glad you decided to move with us.

Besides, Kauehi will not be the same without me there." I heard the grin in his voice.

It was a wonderful day to sail the forty miles from Kauehi to the north pass of Fakarava. I put my fishing line out, hoping to catch something big enough to share with the crew of *Eik*. Just in case, I set up a GoPro too, positioned to watch the fishing line. With the headsail flying and the autopilot running, I sat under the Bimini and watched the waves pass by. As *Welina* angled in for the pass to Fakarava, the fishing lines went off and I wrestled the fish.

I was thrilled to haul in a ten-pound tuna. I posed with it while looking at the camera. "Sushi tonight!" I told my future viewers.

I made my way through the pass, tacking to head directly toward the small town of Rotoava.

Jonas and Eivind came over and helped me pick up a mooring ball as I arrived in the late afternoon. When we were settled, the guys climbed aboard. "Ahoy, Captain," Eivind called out while Jonas tied up their boat. He bounded over and gave me the two European air kisses.

"I have something for you to bring to Marcella," I said to him.

"Oh?"

"In my fridge. Go look."

Eivind disappeared downstairs. "You only get one!" I called.

Jonas climbed back into the cockpit, his dinghy now secure.

We locked eyes and Jonas gave me a slow little grin. Even though we'd just seen each other yesterday, it felt more monumental now. I had chosen to follow him, to stay in his company.

He leaned down and kissed my cheek—not the air kiss I'd gotten from Eivind, but a real kiss, a light brushing of his lips against my skin, a perfect little lean into each other.

"How did things go over on *Eik*?" I asked.

"Ah, beautiful. No problems."

"Oh ho, ho! Look at this beauty." Eivind appeared at the top of the stairs with the bag of fresh tuna. "I better get back before Marcella starts to cook something else for dinner."

While we moved over to the port side and the men climbed in their dinghy, Jonas invited me to join them in town the next day. "We can shop for food, and use the Wi-Fi at the yacht services office. They can also help sort out tours and dives."

"All the important stuff." I grinned. "Sounds good."

"Pick you up at eight," Jonas said as he swung down to the dinghy. He pushed off from *Welina* and started the engine. As I untied their lines, Eivind shouted, "Thanks for the tuna!"

I waved goodbye and headed back into the galley, ready to make my own sushi dinner.

THE FAKARAVA YACHT SERVICES OFFICE WAS A SMALL house with a wooden porch. We weren't the first cruisers to arrive: a couple and a family were already sitting on the chairs, their phones and laptops out.

Jonas disappeared inside to talk to the staff while the rest of us settled into a small round table. I connected to the Wi-Fi and let the notifications ping in.

I ignored my social media accounts for now and checked my personal email. I responded to a few emails from friends, wrote a long email to my sister, Dawn, and logged in to check my bank account.

Moving through the apps on my phone, I read over all the notifications and responded when I wanted to. I pretty much ignored anything having to do with my channel and focused on the personal, lovely things: random hellos from friends and long-winded updates from my close-knit family. There were familial group texts that made me laugh, my siblings and their families in summer shenanigans.

Wrapping things up, I checked in with the *Eik* crew. They had mostly brought their laptops and were working away, brows creased in absolute concentration.

I stood and stretched. "I'm going to go walk around town, check out the stores."

Marcella stood up, dusting her hands off. "I need to shop too. I will join you if it is okay?"

"Sure."

We took off down the road back toward town.

"Do you cook, Mia?"

I scrunched up my nose. "Not well. Certainly not like you do."

"It does help to be professionally trained. What do you like to cook?"

"My mom was a big fan of complicated meals, and I grew up in Seattle where it is usually cold and rainy. I have a fairly extensive repertoire of stews and soups that do me no good here in the tropics."

"Ah yes. You need some light summer soups. Italians are renowned for those."

"Where are you from in Italy?"

"Campania, near Naples. The coast gives us amazing seafood, so that's our specialty, at least in Italy anyway. But I went to the UK to study to be a chef."

"Right. And Lila said you are leaving *Eik*?"

"Yes. When we arrived in Polynesia, I sent out emails to my friends in the industry and several placement agencies. But this morning I got an email from a former colleague, Seb. He was connecting me with a job opportunity. Recommending me, actually."

"Okay."

"And I've slept with him."

"Oooohhhh."

We reached the *magasin*, a small local shop, which was the only place we could buy groceries here. Our conversation took a hiatus as we picked through the fresh produce: rubbery carrots, sprouting onions, green tomatoes.

After finding enough for me for a few days, I walked up and down the aisles of the shop. Everything was canned goods or snack items imported from overseas. I stuffed a few rolls of cookies into my basket and some tins of tuna.

There was a cheese display—we were in French territories, after all—and the cheese was remarkably cheap, stamped with subsidized stickers. I picked out several pieces and paid.

Marcella took a lot longer than me. In the end, I had one bag and she had five large reusable bags full of food, plus a backpack. The baguettes wouldn't fit anywhere, so we stuffed them under our arms.

"It is a good thing I have you with me. Normally I make the men help me."

"So this man. He's recommending you for the job, so it must not have ended poorly, right?"

Marcella adjusted a strap on her shoulder. "It was a one-time thing, but we did get caught, and of course, I got fired."

"Oof. That stinks."

"Yes," she agreed. "So, this is weird, right? Why would he recommend me for the job? And does this person I would be interviewing with know? And if so . . . that doesn't look good for me." Marcella winced. "It is just an interview so far. It's not even a job offer. I may be worrying over nothing." She hesitated.

"What?"

Marcella glanced at me, her eyebrows knitted together. "It's a *really* good job."

"Tell me about it."

Marcella gushed for the rest of the walk about the position. It was for the head chef on a British family's mega sailing yacht. They'd be island hopping, sailing in regattas, and she'd have a substantial budget.

"So, basically, your dream job?"

Her sigh was so disheartened. "Yes."

"Do you have any other prospects?"

"One of the placement agencies said they might

have a job at a charter company. The only other position I've found is a cook-slash-nanny on a smaller sailboat. Both of which I am overqualified for and so I would be underpaid." We made the turn into the driveaway of the yacht services shop and caught sight of the rest of the crew. "But there are some things that are more important than money."

The heat and weight of the backpack had given me a workout on the walk returning to the office, and I was sweaty and sticky when we arrived. Jonas nudged two cold bottles of juice in our direction as we set our groceries down.

Marcella slumped in a chair and knocked back half of her drink in one gulp. Before the bottle left her lips, Eivind had reached over to grab one of the baguettes and he slipped it out of her grip. He broke off a large chunk and passed the rest along.

I took a few sips of my drink. "Here's what I think, Marcella. It's not even a job offer yet, so what harm is there in pursuing it further?"

Marcella pursed her lips in thought and I saw Eivind perk up.

"What is this?"

Marcella told the rest of the crew about the email from Seb, and everyone eagerly agreed she should at least learn more about the job.

"It's unprofessional," she cautioned.

Lila shrugged. "It's life."

Marcella opened her laptop to respond, so I pulled out my phone and refreshed my apps. There was a response back from Dawn already, since it was evening in the States. I typed back another reply, and my finger hovered over the camera roll on my phone. I had transferred the videos from the GoPro over and had a screenshot of me with the tuna. I clicked to share it on Instagram.

Trying to get used to life on board Welina *by myself. It's an ineffable feeling, but then something like this happens, and I can't help but smile. #getinmybelly #sushi-fordinner*

"Mia." I looked up from my phone at Jonas. "We have arranged a pearl farm tour tomorrow. Will you join us?"

"Sure." I'd heard about these tours, one of the biggest attractions in Fakarava—out of the water. The islands were famous for Tahitian pearls, and though I doubted I could afford one, when in Rome . . .

ELEVEN

THE OYSTER TOUR WAS A ROUSING SUCCESS IN THAT I learned two things: how pearls were made, and that Tahitian black pearls were insanely expensive. Our guide had been a big German man who'd married into a local family. His wife ran the shop. Jonas followed me around like a six-foot-tall shadow, and we left without buying anything. Lila and Marcella had lingered. When they finally rejoined us outside the shop, Lila was tucking a small bundle into her bag. Eivind rubbed his belly emphatically.

"Food?"

Marcella rolled her eyes and poked his belly. "Of course, we could have had sandwiches back on the boat, but someone ate all the baguettes we bought yesterday."

"They are better fresh," Eivind protested.

LIZ ALDEN

"There is a café on the way back—let's stop for lunch," Jonas said, playing diplomat.

We detoured to the café and took a seat outside that overlooked the clear blue water. I told Jonas what I wanted from the small menu, and the two men went to the counter to order and pay.

I closed my eyes and basked in the sun for a moment. The pearl shopping combined with checking my bank account balance the other day had me on edge.

Elayna interrupted my thoughts. "The pearls were lovely. You did not want to buy one?"

I looked at her out of the corner of my eye. "No, they are too expensive for my taste."

"They were expensive," Lila agreed. "I only bought a few small, imperfect ones to take home with me. But the jewelry was lovely."

"What will you do for money, Mia? Since you will not be making videos anymore?" Elayna pried.

"I didn't say I wasn't going to make videos anymore. I said I didn't know what I was going to do. I haven't figured it out yet."

"Ah yes, that is right. Well, I'm sure you will think of something."

Jonas and Eivind rejoined our table and Elayna dropped the conversation.

After lunch, we climbed back into the dinghy and

veered off toward the boats. Jonas dropped me off first.

As I unloaded my backpack, I heard the sounds of a dinghy approaching my boat again. Did I forget something?

Jonas pulled alongside *Welina*, and I leaned over to ask what was going on.

He grinned at me. "I am on a secret mission. Come with me."

"Do I need my backpack?"

"No."

I hopped in with Jonas again and we drove off toward land, the engine drowning out any words I might have said.

Once we were tied up again and on dry land, I turned to Jonas. "What is going on?"

Jonas ambled off back toward the oyster farm. "Lila had a favorite piece of jewelry at the shop. I am on a mission to help my brother by buying the ring while she's distracted."

"That's a nice gift for Eivind to give her," I said.

"Ah no, not just a gift. He is proposing."

"He's proposing to Lila?"

Jonas's smile was wide. "Ja, it is exciting, no?"

"Well, yes." I shook my head. "Sorry, yes, it is exciting. I guess I'm still a little . . . burned by the marriage thing. And you are happy about that? Even . . ." I hesitated.

"Even though my marriage failed?" He sobered and thought about it. "Yes, I am happy for them. I know that there are many reasons a marriage goes wrong, but Lila and Eivind have withstood a lot already. The cruising life is hard on couples, but they work together well." He nodded decisively. "It is a good match."

"That's great," I said. It was good to know that while cruising could tank a marriage, it could start one too. As we approached the oyster farm, I thought about the consequences of jumping into a relationship headfirst. I'd known Liam for two years before we got engaged, but clearly, I didn't know him well at all. On the other hand, cruising and the sailing lifestyle had exacerbated the cracks. If Eivind and Lila had already been together for a while, in such conditions, who was I to say whether they would make it or not?

We reached the store and Jonas talked to the shopkeeper. The ring she produced was a beautiful black pearl with silver waves around either side.

Jonas paid and we walked back. "Do you think you'll get married again someday?" I asked. "It sounds like you still believe in marriage."

He looked at me for a moment before answering.

"Yes, I hope someday I can be a better husband than I was before."

I cocked my head. "Why do you say that?"

Jonas sighed and ran his fingers through his hair. It was down and loose, curling around his ears and glistening like silver in the sun.

"It is tough not to think the worst of yourself when you do not really know why your marriage failed."

"You don't know?"

He shook his head. "One day she packed her things and left. Said she did not love me anymore."

I watched Jonas's face for a moment and said carefully, "Do you think there was someone else?"

"I do not think so. She said no."

"Wow. That is hard."

"Did you leave Liam?"

"Yeah, I did."

"What about you? Would you get married again?"

I scrunched up my brow in thought. Finally I said, "I like my freedom."

Jonas nodded, a small frown on his face. "I can understand . . ." He trailed off.

"You can understand what?"

Jonas stopped and turned to face me, indecision in his expression. He ran a hand through his hair and sighed. "I can understand how you can feel that way about marriage. It is tough for me to reconcile this Mia"—he gestured at me—"with the one I know from the videos. I know some of it is that I had known only a small portion of who you are. But I think"—he looked me in the eye—"that some of it is the Mia who's recovering from Liam."

Shame washed over me. I didn't realize that this was how Jonas saw me, like someone who was a little broken. It was true, but hearing the words still caught me off guard. I stepped back, but Jonas followed me and placed his hands on my shoulders. He ducked down, forcing me to meet his eyes straight on.

"I like this Mia better. You may be a little different, but you are tougher, brighter, more real. This Mia I know, she would not be who she is without everything she's been through." He smiled and tugged my ear. "And she will just keep getting better."

My eyes pricked with tears. Jonas's smile faded, and he pulled me into his arms. "Oh, Mia, I am sorry. I did not mean . . ."

I shushed him. "It's okay." I turned my face, pressing closer into Jonas and wiping my eyes. "I feel it too. I'm just not there yet. But I'm working on it."

We pulled back and resumed our walk. When

Jonas dropped me off at *Welina*, it was late afternoon. He said Eivind was proposing that night at sunset.

I sat in the cockpit, keeping an eye on *Eik* and replaying Jonas's words. Being away from everyone I knew felt like I was looking at myself through a filter. I had only my own thoughts and opinions. For months I had been around my family, who loved me and supported me unconditionally. Maybe I was changing in ways that I couldn't see for myself. Maybe cruising alone wasn't a good idea.

A few moments after sunset, I heard whoops and hollers coming from *Eik*. I watched, alone in my cockpit, while the crew of *Eik* celebrated.

———

THE NEXT DAY WE MOVED LOCATIONS. ROTOAVA WAS IN the north of the atoll, but the best snorkeling, quite possibly in all of the South Pacific, was in the south. We departed in the morning and spent the day slowly sailing inside the atoll.

Eik left me behind, but I coasted along under sail, keeping an eye out ahead of me for coral heads and shallow spots, while also watching the shore pass me by. Fakarava was narrower than it was long, and I could clearly see the beautiful beaches and small houses on my left and the breaking waves over the reef on my right all day long.

When I approached the mooring field, Jonas came to help me. He picked up the mooring ball and tied my lines off while I stayed back at the helm.

We were with a small group of boats, and the water below the mooring ball was deep enough that I couldn't see the bottom. But the water was clear and blue, and the beaches on the motus directly in front of us, protecting our anchorage from the ocean swell, were idyllic. White sand and coconut palms stretched out into the distance.

It wasn't quite as remote as we had enjoyed in Kauehi; there was a resort a mile down the motu and several other cruising boats on the mooring balls.

Jonas followed me back to the cockpit. "Tomorrow we go snorkeling. It is a drift snorkel, through the pass here. Will you join us?"

"I would love to." This solved a big problem for me: snorkeling alone, especially a drift snorkel, was dangerous. Being swept out to sea would be a horrible way to die.

"Great. We will pick you up at eight."

I nodded and then surprised myself. Maybe it was because I'd been alone all day, or maybe it was because Jonas was my friend now, but I said, "Would you like to come over for dinner?"

Surprised flashed across Jonas's face. "Just me?"

"Well, you can invite the others if you want—"

"No, no," Jonas interrupted. "Just me. I'll come."

———

THE BOAT NEEDED TIDYING UP BEFORE JONAS CAME OVER for dinner, and I prepared an easy meal of sausages and au gratin and threw it in the oven while I cleaned. The late-afternoon heat combined with the oven meant I was a mess. Feeling sticky and sweaty, I jumped in the water to cool off.

I swam until my timer went off and then, dripping wet, ducked inside and pulled the baking dish out of the oven. I covered it, put it back in, and turned the oven off before stepping back outside to shower.

One of the things I had quickly learned about the cruising community was that Americans were considered prudes. It wasn't uncommon for other sailors to strip off their clothes on the back deck while showering or jump in the clear water completely nude. I'd even seen some men sunbathing or sailing fully naked. Mostly they were older men. I hadn't seen any good-looking Norwegians sunbathing nude yet.

So I didn't hesitate to strip out of my bathing suit

on deck and hang it on the lifelines. I sat on the back and spent a few minutes fastidiously washing my hair, removing as much salt as I could before combing a leave-in conditioner through it.

By the time I was completely ready, Jonas was on his way over. I checked my reflection in the mirror, smoothing down some of the wisps that floated around my face. Having no hair dryer, I was resigned to damp hair, but I'd weaved it into a side braid. No makeup, a tank top and a sarong, and wet hair. A far cry from my first date with Liam, but it was about as dressed up as I could get.

Not that this was a date.

I climbed out of the hotbox that was *Welina* and smiled nervously as Jonas stepped into the cockpit with me. "Hey."

He swung down and handed me a wine bottle, a small smile on his lips. I was pleased to see he'd dressed up a little too, wearing a linen shirt and shorts that were uncharacteristically clean. We were both barefoot, of course.

Jonas leaned in and kissed my cheek. "I was not sure what kind of wine you might like." He held up the bottle.

"Any kind of wine. Let me get some glasses. Stay here—it's hot down below."

With two plastic wineglasses in hand, I returned

to the cockpit. Jonas had grabbed a pillow and curled up in the corner on the port side, prime sunset-watching position. I filled our glasses with the cool white wine while Jonas waited, and then I sat next to him on the bench, handing him his glass.

"*Skål.*" He raised his glass, and I touched mine to his.

"Cheers."

The wine was good—light and sweet. Jonas's free hand caught the end of my braid and tugged. A teasing smile flitted across his lips.

"Your hair is so dark when it is wet."

"I know. Every time I see it, I think about the time I dyed my hair brown as a teenager."

Jonas looked horrified. "You dyed your hair?"

"Yes, well, I was a little rebel in my teenage years, and my hair was just another thing to fight about with my mom. I was tired of my classmates teasing me."

His brow furrowed. "Kids teased you about your hair?" He sounded so genuinely perplexed that I had to laugh.

"Kids will tease about anything."

"Your hair is beautiful," he said so earnestly that it made my heart swoon.

"Well, now I think it's great. It is really pretty, and I remember little old ladies complimenting it, saying they couldn't pay to get my hair color. But kids in my school used to call me names: Carrot Cake, Fire Crotch, and even Ariel, like in *The Little Mermaid*. I mean, at least I can appreciate the irony of that last one now."

Jonas's cheeks flushed pink, and he cleared his throat. "I did, umm, have a big crush on the Little Mermaid when I was a kid." I laughed, and he flushed more, the tips of his ears pink now. "Is that too weird?"

"No. I mean, I have long red hair, and I swim a lot, but sadly I don't have a friend who's a crab." I paused. "I'd probably eat him if I did."

"He would be tasty," Jonas agreed.

I nudged him with my elbow. "Is that why you watched my channel?"

Jonas switched his glass to his other hand and swept his arm behind me, inviting me into his side. "It may be why I clicked on the first video, but not why I stayed. You were fun to watch on camera."

"Thanks. So I should pass on black lingerie and go for a seashell bra and a monofin?" I teased.

Jonas threw his head back and laughed. "Please, no. I like you much better than Ariel." He sipped his wine and pondered something. "Do you own black lingerie?" he asked carefully, a glint in his eye.

I groaned, and it was my turn to blush. Well, I *had* brought it up. "No, I don't. Sorry to disappoint."

He pulled me in close. "I am not disappointed. I get to see you in a bikini all the time."

We sipped our wine and gazed at the sunset. The sky was cloudier than it had been lately, but the clouds were high and wispy, forming pink streaks across the sky. I changed the subject. "Will you tell me what the Northern Lights are like?"

Jonas told me about trips to visit his uncle in the Arctic Circle and camping with Eivind to see the Northern Lights on the outskirts of the city when Jonas was in college. I wasn't surprised to learn that Jonas had taken on the responsibility of raising Eivind to help out their single mother, and had gone to college nearby and delayed his military service until Eivind was old enough to take care of himself.

When it was dark, the colors of sunset washed away, Jonas followed me inside to make our dinner plates. "No wonder you and Eivind are so close," I said as I pulled the dish out of the oven, where it was being kept warm. I handed Jonas an empty plate and gestured for him to help himself.

"Ja. Our mother worked hard as a nurse, but she was rarely home."

"You've been pretty responsible your whole life. Not many teenagers would step up like you did."

"It means Eivind and I are close to each other but not to our mother." I watched him while he scooped up potatoes. "I resent her for it sometimes still."

Back in the cockpit, I switched on some simple solar-paneled lights and fake candles so we could see.

"What about your mom? Are you close to her?" Jonas asked me as he cut into a sausage.

"Yeah, but she was a stay-at-home mom. Hyper-involved in our lives, and I have a big family." Talking about them made my heart pang with home-sickness, so I switched the subject. "Lila told me you work remotely?"

And then we talked about work. Jonas had a degree in engineering and worked for a scientific journal, editing and fact-checking, and I told him about my degree in marketing and the jobs I'd worked after college, aimlessly trying to find something that made me happy. We were slouched together back in the corner now, our plates empty, the wine bottle dry, and the lights out on *Eik*.

I stifled a yawn. It was way past my bedtime. Jonas squeezed my shoulder with the arm he had around me. "Thank you for having me for dinner."

"You are welcome. It's been a long time since I stayed up this late." With no one else around, I'd usually gone to bed early out of boredom. Staying up this late, talking about everything and anything, was something I hadn't done since dating Liam.

Nerves fluttered in my stomach. The night was winding down, and this had felt so much like a date. I sat up and stretched before gathering the plates and glasses, trying to hide awkwardness with activity.

"Can I help?" Jonas asked.

"Why don't you hand this down to me?" I descended the stairs and turned back at the bottom. Jonas handed me the dishes and then stepped down too, resting his arms on the companionway entrance.

I scrubbed the dishes while Jonas waited. He stepped closer and wrapped an arm around my waist.

"Mia," he said gently. "I am going to go back to *Eik*, okay?"

"Yeah?" Tension spooled out of me. "Okay."

He kissed my forehead. "Thank you for dinner. We will pick you up tomorrow for snorkeling, ja?"

"Ja—I mean, yes."

Jonas chuckled and squeezed my shoulder. "Good night, Mia."

"Night."

Jonas climbed the stairs, and a few minutes later I heard the dinghy engine start up.

TWELVE

WHEN THE CREW OF *EIK* CAME BY TO PICK ME UP, I WAS out in the cockpit, ready to go. The high clouds from last night had rolled away, leaving the sky painfully blue and clear. I wore a long-sleeve rash guard and bikini bottoms and I'd slathered on sunscreen and packed the bottle, too. If the snorkeling was as good as they said it was, we would be out there for hours.

"Good morning, everyone."

With a chorus of good mornings, and a soft smile from Jonas, I dropped into the dinghy. He scooted closer to the outboard, trying to make room for me. I sat down and arranged my gear with everyone else's, and we puttered off toward the pass. The tide was incoming, but not full throttle, so we slowly exited out of the pass and into the ocean. Jonas turned right, steering along the edge of the reef, and slowed.

"Our plan is to drift snorkel here along the outer wall," Eivind said as I slipped a weight belt on. "The current will pull us back toward the pass and through it. Jonas will hold the dinghy while we drift along, and if he needs to pass it to me, he will. We'll stick together as best we can, but we will buddy up and stick with our buddies. Jonas and Mia, me and Lila, Marcella and Elayna.

"In the pass, there will be reef sharks. A lot of them, hopefully. It's not quite peak season, but we will see how many there are. When we get far enough inside the atoll, Jonas will get back into the dinghy and fire it up. When you hear that, make sure he sees you before you approach the dinghy. Wave if you need him to drive over and pick you up. Any questions?"

Four snorkel-masked faces shook their heads. Jonas was still maneuvering the dinghy, holding us off the reef, but he spoke up. "Mia, do not dive too deep, yes? None of us can go as deep as you can. Can you stay above ten meters?"

I nodded.

Eivind and Jonas spent some time studying the current and maneuvering the boat into the perfect position.

"Ja?" Jonas asked.

"Ja, looks good," Eivind agreed.

Jonas nodded, killing the engine. "Okay, time to go in!"

Next to me, Elayna pinched her nose through her mask and launched herself backward over the side. Head over heels she splashed in, and when she surfaced, she gave Eivind the all clear signal.

Marcella had gone over the opposite side, so I was next. As soon as Elayna was clear, I tumbled backward, feeling the chill of the water hitting my sun-warmed skin.

I gave Eivind the all clear so he and Jonas could jump in. Putting my face in the water, I took stock of the ocean beneath me and it took my breath away.

To one side was the outer edge of the reef, a straight drop down. The visibility was stunning— easily over a hundred feet, and the ocean floor beneath me went even further. The reef was perfect, colorful and intricate. But that blue of the open ocean? It called to me. The sunbeams cascaded from the surface and little motes of life floated like leaves on a breeze. There was something about staring out into the face of the ocean like this. It humbled me. I knew that I could start swimming and the current would catch me, carry me away, and the last thing I would know was nothing but blue.

I rotated my wrist, pressing a button to engage my dive watch. We were already drifting quickly toward the pass, so I focused my attention on the wall of coral.

Lila swam at the surface to my left, starfished out and drifting with the current. Eivind dove under her, keeping pace in the current about twenty feet under the surface. Elayna and Marcella were ahead of them, Jonas behind me.

With a quick glance back at Jonas, I took a few deep, easy breaths, and tucked and dove. My free-diving fins were longer and hydrodynamic, allowing me to propel myself further. My weight belt helped keep me down, and I didn't have to use as much energy to get there.

I kept an eye on my depth, careful to stay above the agreed-upon ten meters. I leveled out at eight and let the current push me along.

I drifted past sea anemones and their clown fish guards, staghorn coral vibrant with life, and an eel languidly gulping water outside its home. I was down for several minutes before I had to kick up to the surface for air.

When I popped up next to Jonas, I blew hard to clear my snorkel. He looked at me, the corners of his eyes crinkling a bit inside his mask. He gave me the okay signal, which I gave back.

I hadn't seen Jonas dive yet. He held on to the dinghy, but the line was long enough that he could come down a little bit. I hesitated at the surface. I wanted Jonas to experience this too, for him to enjoy the reef as well.

I took a deep inhale and dove below the surface, angling my fins to use my slow, steady strokes to keep me a few feet down, and then I spun around, facing Jonas.

I reached out a hand, beckoning.

Come join me.

His ribs expanded and he tucked and dove. We leveled out together, our bodies close, our arms nearly tangling together. The rest of the group was ahead of us; it was just us in our own blue bubble.

Jonas gripped my forearm and squeezed before he turned and kicked upward to refill his air.

We dove together a few more times, tugging fingers and tapping shoulders to show each other things. Finally the pass came into view and we spotted our first shark. It swam lazily along as I steered into the pass. I dove again and leveled out mere meters from the shark.

He was fairly small; reef sharks only got to be four or five feet long. Another one was below me, and then another, and another. The water clarity meant I could see the whole shiver of them. I looked back up and made eye contact with Jonas at the surface. Even with his mask, I could see the concern in his eyes.

Okay? he signaled me.

Okay.

When I popped up at the surface, Jonas reached for my hand and gave it a squeeze.

The pass spat us out inside the atoll, and the coral started to rise. It leveled out, a plateau of colorful life jigsaw-puzzled together, filling every nook and cranny. It was only ten feet deep now, and we had caught up to Lila and Eivind. I watched her dive, seeing her practicing her technique, and felt a burst of pride. She was pretty good, despite only having gotten a short lesson. I let go of Jonas's hand and joined Lila on her next dive and we drifted together above the coral.

Fish darted in and out of the maze below us and sharks patrolled.

Lila drifted back up to the surface and I felt myself slowing. Now that the pass was done, the ride was over and the current had eased.

Popping up at the surface, I heard the rest of our group laughing and shouting. Jonas climbed into the dinghy to start it, and the rest of us kicked over to pull ourselves aboard.

"Those sharks!" Elayna gasped. "There were so many!"

"It was amazing. I've never seen so much coral in my life." I was giddy with excitement.

"Mia, you are an amazing free diver." Lila grinned at me.

"We go again, ja?" asked Eivind.

Jonas climbed in first and bent over to help me. Getting back into the dinghy wasn't easy by myself, but Jonas braced himself and offered me a hand, pulling me in. Space was tight, so Jonas sat next to me while we shook off the water and arranged our gear out of the way.

Despite the sun beating down, I was chilled from the swim and the droplets of seawater wicked away the heat. I shivered, my skin breaking out in goose bumps.

"Ah, Mia, here." Jonas pulled a towel out of the dry bag and wrapped it around my shoulders. He wrapped an arm around me too and firmly rubbed my upper arm, pulling me into his warmth.

By the time everyone was situated, Jonas fired up the engine and we puttered out to sea again.

The tide was still rolling in, though it would slow as the day went on, so we only had an hour or so before the tide stalled and switched. We rode the current again and again and again.

"One last time," Eivind pleaded.

"There was hardly any current this most recent

time. I think we play it safe and go home. We do not want the tide to switch on us." Jonas, the ever-practical safety officer.

"Nah, yeah. We can go again tomorrow?" Lila was hopeful.

Jonas revved the engine. "We can go tomorrow," he agreed.

We motored home, Jonas dropping me off at my boat first. "See you soon," he said, helping me climb aboard *Welina*. I bit my lip and waved from the deck as Jonas pushed off. We kept smiling at each other as he motored away until Eivind said something and Jonas was forced to turn ahead.

I washed myself and my gear, humming along the whole time. My mind kept getting stuck on the way Jonas had watched me, letting me be myself underwater, a place I always felt more elegant and graceful. I saw it in Jonas too: the lines of his body, contrasted against the deep blue waters, were strong and comfortable.

There had been so much worth looking at.

THIRTEEN

I WAS GOING TO DO SOMETHING I HADN'T DONE IN nearly a year: fly my drone. I'd been looking over the video footage I'd taken since I had relaunched *Welina*, and nothing I had filmed so far did this place justice. I needed to get a view from the air.

So many things were easier to do when I had someone to help me, and flying the drone was one of them. And I knew Jonas would love to get a look "behind the scenes."

After digging out the drone, I plugged the batteries in, emptied the SD card of some old footage, and while I waited for things to charge, I sat at the desk and grabbed the radio.

"*Eik, Eik, Eik,* this is *Welina,*" I called.

"*Welina, Eik,*" Jonas answered, and I could hear his smile coming through.

"Would you like to come over? I could use some help."

"I am on my way." No questions asked.

———

JONAS AND I STOOD ON DECK, MY DRONE SITTING AT OUR feet, ready for flight. I picked it up and handed it to him.

"Here, hold this." I showed him how to grip the legs of the drone and raise it over his head. "It's easier to launch this way because if the boat swings, the drone is already above most of the deck hardware. You ready?"

He nodded, and I started the blades and revved the drone up. Jonas's hair blew against his head, and he squeezed his eyes shut. "Okay, let go!"

Jonas did and I pushed the joysticks to get the drone to fly up and out to sea. The drone hovered over the water, twenty feet or so from the bow, and I peered at the screen of my phone to get oriented.

While I worked the joysticks and positioned the camera just right, Jonas leaned over my shoulder to watch me work.

"Okay, let's get back in the cockpit so we aren't in the shot," I said. Jonas followed me back to the helm and we sat close to each other.

"Have you ever flown a drone before?" I asked him.

"No."

"Do you want to?"

"Ahh . . ."

I grinned at his reluctance. "It's not that scary, I promise. Here."

I handed him the controller and he fumbled to get his grip right.

"Mia! You cannot let me fly your drone! What if I crash it?"

"You'll be fine. It's actually really easy, I promise. The drone I have is a lot simpler than most." I showed him how to make the basic moves, forward, backward, spin the camera.

"Do you have any drone pictures of *Eik*?"

Jonas shook his head, eyes glued to the controls.

"Okay, let's set the altitude for one hundred and twenty feet. That way you'll be above your mast." I showed him how to do it. "Now, set the shot however you want to."

Jonas thought for a minute and then flew the drone over *Eik*. He tried to pivot the camera back to the boat, but couldn't find it. "Mia! Where is the boat? How did I lose the boat?" He was frantically panning the camera around.

I chuckled. "Okay, deep breath. See that map

here?" I pointed at the screen. "That's where the drone is in relation to us. So move the camera slowly back . . . right there. See, there she is!"

Jonas said something under his breath in Norwegian and tried again to get the drone in the right spot. Looking over his shoulder, I could see that he'd framed *Eik* in the shot, and *Welina* was visible behind her.

"You think here?" he asked me.

"Hm. Try backing up a little bit, making the boats smaller. Okay. Now, what about moving a little bit to the left so the boats aren't overlapped? It looks like *Eik* has another mast."

He made the adjustments and I showed him how to take a picture. We worked together to take a dozen photos of *Eik* in the stunning blue waters of the lagoon.

The controller beeped at Jonas. "What did I do?"

I looked at the screen. "Oh, shiitake, the battery is low." Jonas handed me the controller so I could get the drone back to the boat quickly.

"Was it full when we started?"

"Yeah, the batteries don't last terribly long."

"We did not get any pictures of *Welina*."

"That's okay. I have another battery. But I need you to help me land the drone. Go stand on the bow and I'll steer the drone to you. But don't reach for it.

Let it come to you and grab it when it's low enough."

Jonas stood on my bow, his arms outstretched, and waited for the drone to get to him. It beeped at me again. "Yes, yes, I know little guy. We're almost there."

Carefully, with the boat swinging on her anchor, I avoided the rigging and dropped the drone into Jonas's reach.

"Got it," he said.

I shut the blades down and Jonas put it on the deck. "Let me go get the other battery," I said. "I'll be right back."

With the second battery installed, Jonas helped me launch the drone again. This time I kept the controller and took a few more shots of *Welina* by herself and the two boats together. I pressed the record button and filmed my standard shots: panning along the beach, 360-degree rotations around the anchorage, and then it was time for the last shot, a dronie.

"Come here." I gestured for Jonas to follow me to the bow. The drone hovered ahead of us, and I tugged at Jonas until he was exactly where I wanted him. "Okay, stay right there." I bent down and put the controller on the deck. Pressing the special program button, I quickly straightened and slid an arm around Jonas's waist. "Smile and wave!"

He leaned in closer, wrapping his arm around my shoulders and squeezing me in close. I laughed and we both waved at the drone. Three seconds later it tilted and sailed off toward the sky. We stayed still, watching until it was a tiny speck in the blue. Jonas's thumb brushed quickly against my skin and he pulled back.

I bent over and picked up the controller. "This shot is going to be awesome sped up."

"It is surreal for me. I have seen your drone footage so many times, and now I get to see it behind the scenes."

I laughed. "It's nothing special."

"That is not true. Many other YouTubers have lost their drones. You have not lost even one. Right?"

I shrugged. "I've been lucky. Now help me land this thing."

Once the drone was safely on the boat and put away, I pulled out my laptop. "Let's check out our work."

Jonas sat next to me and I transferred the files to my hard drive. He peered over my shoulder as I clicked on the first picture.

He glanced at me before looking at the screen. "It is . . . very gray, no?"

"Oh, right. Yeah, I shot in a gray profile, and we need to add a LUT to the image."

Jonas shook his head. "I do not understand."

"It's technical, I know. Sorry. Hold on."

I opened my photo-editing software and applied the adjustments I needed to make on the first photo. Next to me, Jonas inhaled a sharp breath. "Wow."

I grinned at him. "Our boats look pretty good together, right?"

The pictures were stunning. *Welina* and *Eik* sat in a field of aquamarine that stretched out behind them. I opened all the photos we took, quickly adjusting each one as I went.

"These are amazing." He had me scroll through them again, admiring each one. "Now the videos?"

The video clips took longer to load, but I got them added in the software and we watched the first clip I'd taken.

"It is so slow. Why is that?"

"In my full videos, I usually speed the drone shots up. Otherwise, yeah, they are really slow. Hang on."

I added the dronie clip in and let it play. I watched myself jump up from pressing the button and slide my arm around Jonas. My eyes had been on the drone, so I hadn't noticed it, but Jonas had turned his head and looked at me, and that look . . .

He looked so happy. *We* looked so happy. My hair had been tossed by the light breeze, and my ponytail had flowed over his shoulder. It was a fleeting moment on the screen, but I wanted to watch it again and again to see the way he looked at me.

Jonas was still looking over my shoulder at my laptop, his body a warm weight grazing my back. I heard him swallow, right next to my ear, and a blush warmed my cheeks.

I cleared my throat. "I'll just speed this up to eight hundred percent. See, now it's ten seconds long."

Even without the look, it was ten incredible seconds of footage. By the end, *Welina* and *Eik* were two tiny dots in the lagoon.

"This is amazing," Jonas whispered. I kept working on the photos, cropping, straightening, and adjusting the colors until I had a finished product: one of Jonas's shots of our two boats together.

"Okay, let me get a thumb drive so you can have a copy." I got up and dug through my desk, looking for a drive.

"Can I ask you a question?"

"Sure."

"I heard you say *shiitake* today, and in a lot of your videos. And a few other words, curse words but not. You do not say *fuck* or *shit*?"

I glanced back at him and laughed. "No, I don't.

Well, not usually anyway. I have a bunch of niblings, so I've gotten used to not saying curse words."

"Niblings?"

"Collective gender-neutral noun for my siblings' kids. Aka nieces and nephews."

"Ah, so you are an aunt."

"Yes, many times over."

Jonas settled back and put his feet on the couch. "Tell me about your family."

I finally found a thumb drive I was willing to part with. I plugged it in and started the file transfer.

"Well, it's big. I have five siblings, but not unsurprising, I'm closest to my younger brother, James, and Dawn, my only sister. But between my four oldest siblings, there are ten, soon to be eleven, kids. So ever since my nephew Tyrell was born, there have been kids around."

"So you say *shiitake*? And *fudgsicles*, ja? What else?"

"*Biscuits* instead of *bitches*. Sometimes *fluffernutter* is a good substitute for *motherfucker*."

Jonas tsk-tsked at me. "The mouth of a sailor."

Suddenly I heard a dinging sound nearby.

Jonas looked up. "What was that? Your satellite phone?"

I frowned. "Yes, I think so."

I maneuvered myself out from the couch and

stood at my navigation station. The satellite device was mounted on the wall near the rest of my electronics.

Pressing the button on the front, I saw that I did, in fact, have a new message. It must be my family—speak of the devils. I sat and connected my phone to the network.

I had a message from my oldest brother.

Call me when you can.

Hmm. It was unusual for Doug to reach out to me.

I hated calling back home on the satellite phone. There was always a lag, and we were constantly talking over each other with a terrible connection. I was better at it than my siblings, who always got impatient and kept saying, "Hello? Hello? Mia?" Nevertheless, I opened the app to make calls and dialed.

"I have to call my brother real quick."

Jonas tilted his head at me and nodded. I gestured for him to make himself comfortable.

I hit the call button and put the phone up to my ear. It was silent for several long moments, and I waited patiently. Then I heard the rings—most of them only partial while the connection tried to work itself out.

I heard the click and Doug said hello.

"Hey, Doug."

I waited three seconds for Doug's response.

"Hi, Mia! Where are you?"

"I'm at an island called—"

"Mia? Hello? Can you hear me?"

I sighed.

"Doug, I'm here. There's a—"

"Oh, there you are."

"—lag. It'll take a few minutes—"

"Okay, I can hear you now."

I snapped my mouth shut and waited.

"Mia?"

"Yes, I'm here."

Come on, Doug.

"Okay, I can hear you now. Can you hear me?"

"Yes, Doug, I can hear you."

Three seconds.

"Where are you, baby sister?"

"Fakarava."

Three seconds.

"Where is that? Are you near Tahiti?"

"Close."

Three seconds.

"Good, good. I'm sure it's beautiful."

"It is really nice out—"

"Listen, Mia, I've got some bad news— What?"

I rolled my eyes and gritted my teeth.

"What's the bad news?" *Couldn't we have texted?*

"Grandma passed."

And just like that my frustration melted away, shock hitting my heart. "Oh no." Jonas looked up at the change of tone in my voice. I collapsed onto the bench next to me and covered my face with my hand. Out of the corner of my eye, I saw Jonas approach me, and the weight of his hand rested on my shoulder, squeezing me in concern.

"Mia, this connection is terrible. Did you get that? Grandma died?"

"Yeah—yeah, I did."

"I'll email you some details, okay? Check your email tonight."

"Will do. Thanks for ca—"

"Gotta go. Love you, Mia."

I ended the call and set the phone on the table. Jonas crouched next to me.

"Is everything okay back at home with your family?"

"My grandma died."

Jonas took my hand in his. "Ah, Mia. I am so sorry."

I blinked. "It's . . . Well, it's okay. I'm okay. She was old."

"How old was she?"

"Let's see . . . ninety-four? I think that's right.

She's had dementia for a while, and last time I visited, she didn't know who I was. Who any of us were, actually. She thought Doug was my dad." My eyes filled. I was so lucky to have been able to spend time with her while she was alive, but time was the one thing we couldn't buy, and now I'd lost any chance of seeing her again.

"Come sit."

Gently, Jonas tugged me out from behind the desk and led me to the love seat on the port side. He sat and pulled me next to him, holding me close to his side. I was stunned, bombarded by my emotions as tears slid down my cheeks. Jonas held me carefully until I could talk again.

"Crackers," I began. "That's my grandma—she was pretty healthy physically until a couple of months ago. And I guess I hadn't had an update in a while, so I thought that things were a bit better."

Jonas rubbed circles on my back, kneading the muscles and comforting me at the same time. "Why do you call her Crackers?"

"Oh God." I laughed through my clogged throat. "She was always a pretty thrifty lady, like most people who grew up post–Great Depression. She always had crackers in her purse that she'd stolen from the local diner, and my nephew Sean *loved* those crackers. Whenever he saw her, he'd ask for crackers right away and the name stuck."

As I talked more about my grandmother, I leaned into Jonas more. He was so warm and comfortable, and at a time when I felt so far away from everyone I loved, I needed something to ground me. He listened patiently, grabbed tissues for me when I needed to blow my nose, and when I was all tired out, he made me a cup of tea. My satellite device had pinged a few times, so I had Jonas turn it off for me. The pull to my family was calling, but a few choppy phone calls or text messages weren't as comforting as Jonas.

The sky through *Welina*'s portholes had darkened with the approaching evening. I sipped my tea and finished telling Jonas about the birthday party my grandmother had thrown for me when I was twenty-five.

"Crackers kept telling everyone who would listen —waitstaff, other patrons, my friends—that she was so proud of her 'working girl.' Of course, James teased me about it mercilessly. And my dad too." I laughed and tilted my head back against the seat.

"Your family sounds so close. And . . ."

"Big?"

He smiled at me. "I was going to say rowdy."

"That too."

Jonas played with his own mug, flipping the tea

tag around. "Will you go back home? To be with your family?"

"Yeah, probably. I can't afford it, but my parents will insist on me flying back and them paying. It's hard to get the whole family together at the same time, and I haven't seen some of my siblings in a while. And it's summer, so it'll be easier since the kids aren't in school."

I tilted my head to look at Jonas, and I saw the sadness in his eyes. If I was flying back home, it was likely we would be parting for good soon. I didn't know what any of my options were yet, but I doubted that the next few weeks would be easy.

Jonas brought his hand up to my cheek and stroked softly with his thumb. Suddenly I wasn't thinking about how difficult it could be. Instead I wondered if Jonas would stay with me tonight. The idea of being alone seemed awful.

My eyes flicked down to his lips and then back up. His eyes changed, the softness and concern in them growing to something different, something bigger.

But that something scared me and made me pull back. It wasn't right to use Jonas like that for comfort; it was too risky for both of us.

Jonas saw something in my eyes and flicked his

gaze away. I rolled my head to his shoulder and sighed. "Thank you for taking care of me."

He turned back and pressed a kiss to my forehead. "Anytime."

By unspoken agreement we stood up and with one last hug, Jonas went home.

FOURTEEN

THAT NIGHT I CHECKED MY EMAILS AND HAD ONE FROM nearly each of my siblings and one from my mom. Doug had emailed me more details: Crackers had slipped away peacefully in the night, with no suffering, which gave me more comfort.

Doug said he thought he'd organize holding the service in a couple of weeks. I desperately wanted to be there, but planning to get there would be a pain.

I messaged back and forth with James, who often helped me when I was away from proper internet. On the satellite device, I couldn't actually browse the internet; I could only send and receive small text-based emails or messages. James looked up flight information for me, sending me several options. I pulled up my charts.

Looks like the best option is via LAX, James wrote. *Only three flights a week.*

From Tahiti? I have to get there first. What are my options? I think there's an airport here in Fakarava.

No ferry. Flights 4x a week. Ugh, you'd have to overnight in Tahiti. So that's like . . . another day of travel.

Actually, can you look up marinas in Tahiti?

While James researched for me, I pulled out my charts and downloaded weather files. If I could make it to Tahiti . . .

My phone pinged.

Several marinas. I have contact info. Want me to check availability?

I chewed on my lip. It was over two hundred and seventy miles from here to Tahiti, and I would have to do that in a two-night trip, sailing by myself. But I didn't want to leave *Welina* here unattended. My entire home and possessions were on board, and something as simple as an ill-maintained mooring ball could cause my entire life to turn upside down.

James emailed the Tahiti marina on my behalf, and there was nothing to do but wait till they responded.

By that time it was late for me, and exceedingly late for James. I ate a can of soup and sat in my main salon, laptop on the table in front of me. I clicked through my photos, feeling nostalgia and sadness taking over. There was Crackers at her ninetieth birthday party, at my wedding, as a young coed, bright-eyed and beautiful.

I collapsed on the pillows around me and cried myself to sleep.

———

I HAD SLEPT POORLY, AND SELFISHLY THOUGHT THAT perhaps if Jonas had stayed, if we'd changed our relationship irrevocably, maybe I would wake up feeling something other than loneliness.

When I got up, I had an email from James, forwarding an email from one of the marinas in Tahiti. Yes, they could fit *Welina* in at the dock.

This was not the marina in Papeete, but the marina on the south side of the island, further away from the city but cheaper, larger, and more popular with sailors.

Now I had to figure out how to get there. My heart felt like lead in my chest when I thought about sailing to Tahiti by myself. It would be my first overnight alone, covering so many miles. I checked the weather forecast, which was . . . okay . . . for the next few days.

I was interrupted by a knock on my hull. I walked up the stairs and found Jonas climbing on board, holding a packet of aluminum foil.

"Hey," he said softly, and kissed my cheek. "This is from us. Well, really, it is from Marcella, but from us all too."

"Thank you." I took the packet in my hands and peeled the edge back, looking inside. "Coconut cupcakes?"

He nodded. "And . . ." I looked where he pointed and found a husked coconut sitting on my back deck.

I smiled at Jonas. "Did you find a new stake somewhere?"

He tilted his chin out to the small guesthouse on the motu. "I bought it at the bar there."

"Aw. Thank you, that's very kind." I sniffed the cupcakes and looked mischievously at Jonas. "Breakfast?"

He laughed and we went into the salon. I had papers from my planning notes strewn everywhere.

"What is all this?" Jonas took an enormous bite of a cupcake.

"I am trying to figure out where to go. I don't really want to leave the boat here in Fakarava."

"Where can you leave the boat?"

"I think . . . I think I will have to go to Tahiti. This

is not secure here, and I would rather be in the marina."

Jonas nodded. "When do you have to leave?"

I shrugged. "Probably sooner would be better. James is helping me arrange flights and I'll worry less with *Welina* in a marina."

"I can keep an eye on her."

I cocked my head at him. "You are ready to leave for Tahiti too? Your crew seems to be really enjoying it here."

He hesitated. "We have done everything we want to do here. The islands have been amazing, but we do need to move on soon. I have to look ahead to the end of the season."

"Oh. What do you think of the weather?"

"I have not looked at it."

"Here, it's on my laptop." Jonas sat at my desk and took over the mouse, looking at the weather patterns and systems that were forecasted for the next few days. I bent over his shoulder, my hand on the desk, as he made changes and scrolled through the time charts.

"What do you average?"

"About five and a half knots, maybe six, if I motor sail."

He grunted and I smiled.

"Do I even want to know how fast you go?"

His lip quirked up. "Seven knots. Maybe eight with the wind on the beam like these conditions."

I sighed. "I bet she's beautiful under sail."

Jonas turned around in the chair, bringing our faces closer together. His eyes darted down and back up quickly. I straightened, realizing that Jonas had had a view right down my braless tank top.

His cheeks flushed, and before I could say anything, he changed the subject.

"This will be your first overnight sail by yourself, yes?"

I bit my lip. "Yeah."

"How do you feel about it?"

"Well . . ." I hedged. Jonas watched me expectantly. "I don't feel great about it."

He stood up and corralled me back to the love seat. "What are you worried about?"

I covered my face with my hands and took some deep breaths. "I'm a good sailor, I know that. But I just have this little voice in my head." Despite all the crying I'd done lately, I felt tears well up in my eyes again. I squeezed them shut. "And I don't want to tell you this, because I feel like I'll be letting you down."

"Ah, Mia . . ." Jonas gently pulled my hands away from my face and I looked up at the ceiling. "Mia, look at me." He nudged my chin until I turned to look at him.

"It's not just you," I admitted. "I know my family is just trying to be supportive. They're all like, 'You can do it, Mia!' 'Go kick ass without Liam!' So it just feels like . . . It feels like if I quit, not only do I lose the hope of doing something that I love, but I also let people down."

Jonas hummed sympathetically.

"It's just that solo sailing was never what I signed up for. And I just . . . I just *don't want to.*" I tucked my head into Jonas's neck and he wrapped his arms around me. "I know it's not sustainable. I'm going to have to do this someday, but I just don't feel like I'm back on my feet yet."

"And that is okay." He rubbed my arm. "You will be someday, and if today is not that day, that is okay."

"Yeah, well." I laughed darkly. "I don't have much of a choice. I want to be there for my family."

"What if I sailed with you?"

"What?" I drew back and looked up at him. "Jonas, no, I can't ask you to do that."

He grabbed my hand. "I want to do it. I will help you, okay? Eivind can manage my boat fine."

"Are you sure? Wouldn't that be weird for you?"

Jonas chuckled. "Yes, I am sure. When do you want to leave?"

I suddenly felt lighter and the prospect of sailing to Tahiti, with Jonas, became something to look forward to instead of something to dread. "We can leave tomorrow. I'll be ready then."

Nodding, he stood up. "Today it is our last day in Fakarava, yes? Let's go snorkeling again."

FIFTEEN

EIVIND DROPPED JONAS OFF AT *WELINA* EARLY IN THE morning, and Jonas brought with him a small duffel bag full of clothes and his own deck harness. He stepped aboard and handed me a container of strawberry jam pastries, a gift from Marcella. Even though *Welina* was so much slower than *Eik*, we were leaving together to exit the pass at slack tide.

I had coffee ready, and Jonas and I ate our breakfast in the cockpit as Eivind raised their dinghy and the rest of the crew puttered around on deck, preparing the boat for the short passage. I had already tackled a lot of things last night while I couldn't sleep, so *Welina* was nearly ready to go.

I shifted around on the cushion, sipping my coffee. Jonas completely absorbed himself with the pastry, relaxed and comfortable. I wondered if he was worried at all about leaving his crew on their own.

After preparing some food—a pasta salad—last night, I'd checked the weather again and emailed more with my brother. The marina was expecting me, and James had booked my flight for me. I left in four days. That gave me plenty of time to arrive in Tahiti.

Jonas ate his last bite of pastry and licked his fingers clean. I stared, trying to distract myself from the building excitement in my stomach. Two nights of sailing out in the open ocean was going to be amazing, but also, the prospect of spending that much time with Jonas thrilled me.

"What can I do to help?" Jonas asked, his expression open and eager. Liam had always been a bundle of stress before every passage, and it swelled my heart that Jonas was so eager to sail with me.

I blew out a breath and blinked, focusing on his face. "Let's go talk through the lines and sail setup together and then we can go through the safety checklist so you know where everything is."

We went downstairs and I sat at my desk. We read the list out loud and ticked off the tasks I'd already accomplished. "Check VHF, check electronics, bring out headsails, secure the dinghy . . ."

The few ones that were left were easy to tackle as we got underway.

We were discussing the sails on *Welina* when my VHF crackled.

"*Welina, Welina, Eik.*"

I picked up the handset. "*Eik, Welina,* up one?"

"Up one."

I changed the channels and hailed *Eik*.

"Are you ready to go?" Eivind asked.

"Roger that, see you out there."

I switched back to channel sixteen and Jonas and I climbed into the cockpit. I fired up the engine and checked the electronics. Jonas cast us off the mooring ball and we motored toward the pass.

Eik cast off too, and when I turned to look back, I could see the crew on deck, Eivind at the helm.

Jonas stood beside me as I pointed *Welina* out toward the pass. The day was still early, the sun not quite out fully, so the visibility wasn't the best, but this pass was well charted and open.

"Does it feel weird not being on *Eik*?" I asked Jonas.

He looked out over the water and grinned. "I will be interested to hear how Eivind does with the responsibility." He stretched, closing his eyes and leaning way back. His shirt rode up, a sliver of skin flashed. "I feel . . ."

I tilted my head, mesmerized by the sight of

muscles flexing and a light dusting of hair. "What?" I laughed when he trailed off with a big smile.

"You are the boss now. I will do as you wish."

I raised an eyebrow. "Shall I make you swab the deck? Polish the stainless? Get to work, cabin boy."

He opened his eyes and hummed.

"The current looks good," Jonas said, pointing to my electronics, which read a speed against us of less than half a knot. Taken at the wrong time, these passes could have a tidal rip running through them, four knots or more. I relaxed my grip on the wheel, glad that I'd gotten the timing right.

Jonas stripped off his shirt, and in only his shorts walked to the bow of *Welina* as we entered the pass. He gripped the bow rigging, leaning over the edge and looking down into the pass. I could picture it as we'd seen it while snorkeling: clear water and the colorful trench, crusted with coral on either side.

My depth meter read thirty feet, so I didn't need Jonas at the bow, but I envied his view. Although my view was lovely too: Jonas's long light hair pulled back in a ponytail, his strong shoulders and tanned skin a contrast against the deep blue waters around us and the clear sky above.

We chugged along, and my depth sounder dropped: fifty, one hundred, nothing. The ocean was too deep here for the sounder to read. We'd finished the pass.

Jonas climbed back into the cockpit and grinned at me. "Ready to get the sails up?"

I nodded and switched the autopilot on. We climbed to the deck together and prepared the main. It felt weird to do this with Jonas. He worked quietly alongside me, letting me lead and instruct him on how to handle my boat.

With the mainsail completely up, I steered her off, pointing our bow toward Tahiti. Jonas worked the jib out, and we picked up speed. I turned the engine off and the autopilot on. *Welina* smoothed out, gliding quickly through the water.

Eik was nearby, clear of the pass too. They had been faster getting their sails up and were already moving along quickly. It wouldn't be long before they were out of sight.

"This is actually the first time I've gotten the mainsail up without Liam."

"You did well."

I sat back, listening to the quiet hum of the boat. The sails creaked and groaned; the waves slashed gently against the hull.

I had forgotten how peaceful sailing could be. I'd been on board *Welina* alone for weeks now, never experiencing the pleasure of clipping along under full sails. I could feel the joy radiating off my boat.

Jonas sat next to me on the bench. "How do you want to do watches tonight?" he asked.

I tilted my head in thought. "Dinner is made, so no cooking tonight. Why don't I take the first watch and we will do six-hour shifts. So I'll take my watch now and you can sleep or whatever until after lunch."

"Ja. That is a good plan." He grinned at me. "I will go get my book. Can I get anything for you?"

I shook my head. "I'm good, thank you."

Jonas returned a few minutes later with his book and a tumbler of coffee. He set my book on the helm seat and winked at me. "Just in case."

I sat by the helm while Jonas settled in to read. *Eik* was growing smaller and smaller on the horizon.

The morning was uneventful. *Eik* hailed us on the radio every hour until they passed out of range. Jonas dozed, lulled by the rocking motion of the boat. Sometimes I watched him, his pale eyelashes fluttering as he dreamed.

Around noon he shifted more, blinked his eyes open, and did a full-body stretch, arms extended above his head, his rib cage expanding and his toes pointing out over the back of the bench. He was too tall to fit fully stretched out in my cockpit, and I wondered if his own cockpit was big enough.

He scratched his belly and smiled at me. Sitting up, he touched a finger to the tip of my nose. "Lunch?"

"That sounds good."

He didn't ask what was for lunch, and I let him wander down into my boat unsupervised. Drawers opened, utensils clicked, and Jonas came up a few minutes later with a bowl of tuna salad and crackers. I was running dangerously low on crackers—heck, I was dangerously low on a lot of things. It was really a good thing we were headed to Tahiti. Though I could have delayed it, it would be nice to hit the big Carrefour supermarket and stock *Welina* again.

"Your big family." Jonas swallowed his bite. "It is unusual for an American, ja?"

I nodded. "While we are no longer practicing, my dad's family was Irish Catholic, so he's always had a big family and wanted the same."

"You are closest to James?"

I smiled. "Maybe not as close as you and Eivind, but yes, pretty close."

"He came to stay on the boat for a little while, ja? I think I remember a video in . . . Mexico?"

I grunted. "That did not go over well. Small

spaces and James don't work very much, and adding in Liam was a disaster."

Jonas nodded in sympathy. "Families are tough."

"You said you aren't that close to your mom? How does she feel about having both her sons out sailing?"

"She is supportive, but she is alone and getting older. I worry because we are not there. It is part of a reason to go now: she will need caretaking before too long."

I nodded and took another bite. Many sailors worried about their families. Some had aging parents or grandparents to care for. Or, on the other side of the spectrum, there were kids to consider, and pregnancy often meant moving back to land life.

"What is the plan when you get to New Zealand?"

"I will sell the boat. I cannot ask Eivind to go further, especially now that he has Lila. They are great to have, but sailing is not something they want in their future."

"You won't sail by yourself on your big beautiful boat?" I teased.

Jonas chuckled. "It is too much."

"You could get more crew. You'll be replacing Marcella, right?"

"We have been lucky with our crew. I will never

find another crew member like Marcella or Elayna." He struggled with his words a bit. "I do not like it so much. I had always wanted to sail away with a partner, or a wife. To take on strangers, and worry about their safety or your own safety, your boat . . ." He shook his head. "It is too much."

"That makes sense. It is hard. You have to really trust your crew, I would imagine. It should be easier when it's your partner, someone you know really well, and can anticipate them."

Jonas watched my face. "It should be, ja. But not always, no?"

I stared out at the sky behind him. "No, not always."

The conversation hung for a moment till Jonas broke the silence. "You should sleep if you can."

"Yes, I should." I gathered our lunch plates and put them in the sink below. When I came back up, I gave Jonas a briefing. He was already familiar with the electronics system, so my briefing was short.

"I might sleep out here if that's okay with you?"

"Of course. I will take good care of your boat, though, if you will sleep better downstairs."

I shook my head. "I like the fresh air." I curled into the corner on the bench and read for a little bit until sleep overtook me.

SIXTEEN

I woke to Jonas sitting at my feet. He was reading and absentmindedly stroking the top of my foot while *Welina* meandered along under full sails.

When Jonas looked up, he smiled at me and I grinned back. Just like he had, I stretched deeply and yawned. My toes pointed, and the flexing of my muscles caused Jonas's hand to slip further up my calf. I faced the back of the bench and wedged myself in.

Jonas chuckled and resumed running his fingers over my skin. It didn't tickle me like it should have. It felt good, and I was loath to stop him.

Checking the time, I saw that I had slept away most of the afternoon. Rolling off the bench, I forced myself to go downstairs and make a coffee. I braced my hands against the furniture or walls as I walked around, struggling to get used to the motion again. It had been so long since I'd felt the boat move like this. When I was done, I climbed back into the cockpit, sitting in the corner and kicking my feet into Jonas's lap. We read in silence while *Welina* sailed along, and to my pleasure, Jonas resumed stroking my feet. I was so comfortable, I dozed off again, despite the caffeine.

When I woke up, the sun was a few fingers away from the horizon and I couldn't see Jonas anywhere. I sat up, looking around. "Jonas?" I called out.

"Down here," came his voice from the main salon. "I am preparing dinner. Would you like to eat?"

My stomach rumbled. "Yes, please."

A few minutes later Jonas stuck his head out and handed me two bowls of pasta, then waters, utensils, and napkins.

We ate, watching the sun creep down the sky.

"On *Eik* we have a tradition."

"Yeah?"

"We all watch the sunset together. Usually, we have just eaten, and it is a very peaceful part of the night."

I looked at him. "Will you stay and watch the sunset with me?"

He flashed me a smile. "Of course."

Dinner finished, we sat back and watched the

sunset, the clouds building layers of color. The ocean, normally a lapis blue, reflected the sunset back at us.

"You started sailing when you were young, ja?"

I nodded. "At summer camp. It was my favorite activity, and when I came home, my dad took me to the local sailing club. My brothers were a bit too undisciplined, and they got discouraged when I always beat them around the courses."

Jonas grinned. "Even the older ones?"

"Even the older ones. They didn't enjoy it quite like I did, so they hadn't paid enough attention to really sail well."

"But you kept up with it."

"I did. What about you?"

"I always wanted to be out in the ocean. But I never got the opportunity to be out on a sailboat until I was older."

"I can't picture sailing as a popular sport in Norway, maybe because of the seasonality."

He chuckled. "No, it is not. But it makes it more appreciated. The people who have boats take them out in the summer and really enjoy the sailing."

I leaned my head back against the bench and looked at Jonas. He was watching me, legs bent and arm resting on the deck. "It must be beautiful there. I can't even imagine what it's like. I've been in the tropics too long."

"It is frigid."

"Will you go back?"

"Ja. But I will miss *Eik*. I will have to buy something smaller."

The bottom of the sun touched the horizon, the gold melting into a puddle above the sea. Jonas extended his arm behind me, his fingertips barely grazing my bare shoulder.

We watched the sun dissolve until it disappeared.

"You should go sleep," I said.

Jonas kissed my cheek and disappeared below.

My watch was peaceful, the moon setting midway through my shift. The stars stretched out overhead, tracing a path to Tahiti.

I occasionally tweaked the sails, responding to the wind and keeping us on course, but the winds were light enough that we cruised along without any major work.

A few minutes before one in the morning I saw flashes of red light in the salon, and it wasn't long before Jonas was up. Wearing his harness and headlamp, he greeted me with a kiss on the cheek and then a big yawn as he sat.

He sipped from a mug while I told him about our sail plan. I let him play with the electronics a bit, check all the sails and lines before I disappeared below.

I pulled my harness off and brushed my teeth, bracing against the sway of the boat. To keep things simple, I stripped my pants off and climbed into bed in my shirt and underwear.

Sitting back on my heels, I looked at the bed. Jonas had slept here. A flattened palm on the sheet told me that the bed was no longer warm from his body. Like a weirdo, I pressed my face into the bed, one side and then the other. The right side, the side I usually slept on, smelled faintly of him.

I smiled and snuggled into the sheets. The rocking of *Welina* put me to sleep quickly.

————

I woke up in the morning with strong sunlight shining into my cabin. The boat creaked and groaned around me, sailing along well. I slid out of bed and, carrying a cup of coffee upstairs with me, joined Jonas.

He allowed me the time to wake up and then gave me a briefing, heading downstairs to nap while I took over.

A few hours into Jonas's nap, I was reading on the bench, nearly done with my book, when an alarm went off downstairs.

My head snapped up—I knew that alarm. It was

the automatic bilge pump, meaning that water was being pumped overboard from inside the boat. *Welina* was taking on water. I scrambled down the stairs, just in time for Jonas to come out of the cabin, dressed in briefs and looking bleary-eyed but waking up quickly.

I froze, panicked. Instead of all the things I knew I should be thinking about—what steps I should take to identify the source of the water and clog the leak—I couldn't stop thinking about that time with Liam. The alarm had gone off, we'd panicked, and everything had spiraled until we were yelling at each other. I couldn't even remember how we'd stopped the leak, but I did remember that, at the end of the day, I'd slept alone, tossing and turning in the bunk, my wrist throbbing too much to let me sleep.

That day, the way he'd grabbed my arm, was the beginning of the end.

"Mia?" I heard softly. "Mia." My eyes came back into focus and there was Jonas, eyebrows bunched in concern and his fingers gently brushing my cheek.

"What can I do to help?"

I blinked, trying to scrub Liam's angry face from my memory. Instead of fear, panic, or anger, I focused on Jonas's sweet smile and kind eyes.

"It's the bilge pump," I said carefully.

"Okay."

That was the only response I got. No yelling—just a calm and stoic Jonas watching me while pulling his harness on.

"Heave us to."

Jonas nodded and climbed the stairs to the cockpit. While I opened all the floorboards, I listened to Jonas adjust the sails. With our headsail backwinded, *Welina*'s speed dropped instantly.

When he came back down, I was looking into the bilges, thinking. The alarm still screeched around us, and it would keep going until the pump died or there was no water left to pump out. "The bilge pump isn't keeping up with the ingress, but it's close. There's a manual pump under the settee. Can you use it and pump the water into the galley sink?"

Jonas started disassembling the salon couch. I dipped a finger into the water of the bilge and brought it to my mouth.

Were we flooding or sinking? The water tasted salty—not good. If the water was fresh water, we would be flooding, the water coming from somewhere in the freshwater system. Instead the boat was sinking, the water coming from outside going in.

Jonas had the manual pump set up and was aggressively pumping water out to the galley sink, where it drained overboard.

"I'm going to close the thru-hulls," I said. Jonas

nodded again, his brow wrinkled in concentration and sweat beading on his temples.

One by one, I quickly went through each valve in the bilge. There were only eight thru-hulls on *Welina* that were under the waterline—holes that could be the source of a saltwater leak. Each hole had a hose and a valve to close it.

When I finished the last valve, I sat back on my heels and crossed my fingers, hoping that would solve the problem.

Jonas was still pumping and the automatic bilge pumps were still going. I stared at the water level in my boat. It *should* be going down. *Please be dropping.*

Though *Welina*'s speed was greatly reduced, the boat still rolled around in the open ocean. It took several minutes for me to realize that the water level was indeed going down.

I glanced at Jonas. With one end of the pump in the bilge, and the other end in the sink, Jonas was working the pump one-handed. His body was completely soaked in sweat.

"I think you can stop now." Jonas halted his movements and sat back, wiping his forehead and pushing his hair out of his face.

We watched the water level. In a few minutes, the automatic bilge pump should have finished the rest of the work for us.

With every swish of the water, I kept changing my mind—*it's rising; no, it's dropping*. The automatic bilge pump still chugged along, the alarm kept ringing.

"I think it is rising," Jonas remarked.

Damn it. "I think so too." This was not going to be an easy fix. "I'm sorry to do this to you, but if we can get the water level down as far as possible with the manual pump, we should."

Jonas got back to work. I grabbed a cup and bailed as much water as I could into the same sink.

The minutes felt like hours, and Jonas and I swapped so I could use the manual pump and give him a break. The water was dropping—slowly but surely.

Finally the bilge alarm turned off. Jonas took the manual pump from me and I grabbed a headlamp and shoved my head into the bilges one by one, looking around for any obvious leaks. The bilge was broken up into several compartments, so I wedged a plug in the holes between the compartments to try to see where the water was coming from.

I was about to duck out of one of the larger compartments when a flash caught my eye. Bending down into the bilge, I reached out to grip one of the hoses and I saw it again: the flash of my light reflecting off water.

Fingering the hose, I found water pouring from a crack on the opposite side of the hose. When the boat surged to one side, the water gushed out, catching the light from my headlamp.

This, I knew how to fix. In a few minutes, I had a silicone tape wound around the hose and I watched it carefully for a few minutes. No gushing.

The tension swept entirely out of my body. I collapsed against the floor and laughed darkly.

"I can't believe I figured it out! We aren't sinking!"

Jonas laughed beside me, placing a hand on my thigh. "You did great. I am impressed, Captain."

I laughed again, a little more freely this time.

Jonas and I got the sails set again and *Welina* pointed back on course to Tahiti. I checked the horizon and radar—nothing to see. We still had to clean up the water that remained in the bilge, the water too low for the pump to get, and the mess we'd made on the floorboards. We worked together, running chamois around the surfaces and squeezing the water out into buckets to dump overboard.

Crisis averted and boat cleaned, Jonas and I collapsed into a sweaty heap. We'd missed lunch by an hour or so, and I was sweaty, tired, thirsty, and hungry. I didn't know whether to eat or pass out.

Jonas's rumbling stomach made the decision for

me. I gripped the table and pulled myself off the couch, swaying my way into the galley to make lunch. It was the last of the pasta salad, so I scooped it into bowls and grabbed spoons. Jonas ate hungrily, helping himself to a stack of crackers when he finished.

He sighed, leaning back against the cushions. When he closed his eyes, I poked him. "Go shower."

Jonas didn't argue, but stood and made his way back to the cabin. He didn't bother closing the cabin door before he stripped his underwear off. My hand froze on the way to my mouth, spiral noodles dangling from the tines of my fork. His butt cheek was white, a gradient tan line working down his thigh. His glute muscle flexed as he kicked his underwear clear, and when he turned to open the door to the head, I swear I saw his dick swing into my view.

He disappeared into the head, and in a few moments I heard the water run. I stared at where he'd been standing, my body a confused mix of exhausted, cranky, and turned on.

SEVENTEEN

AFTER WE HAD BOTH SHOWERED, I TRIED TO GET JONAS to take a nap, but he insisted on sticking to the schedule, which meant it was my nap time.

I had lain in bed, still a bit high on the adrenaline rush. My boat had *been sinking*. And I'd rescued it. And it hadn't been a chaotic, loud mess. I thought back to all the other times when something had gone dangerously wrong out at sea on *Welina*: a broken line, a sail unfurling and beating in the wind, squalls rolling through that tripled the wind speed in a matter of minutes. Those memories were full of yelling and crying.

Instead I was lying in my cabin, a scary moment behind me, and I'd come out the other end better for it.

———

I DID, EVENTUALLY, DRIFT INTO A NAP. WHEN I WOKE up, I found Jonas at the helm, slightly groggy but awake. I made us sandwiches and he scarfed his down. With a kiss on my temple, Jonas apologized for missing the sunset, turned tail, and crashed down below. I couldn't blame him.

The second night out at sea was always the worst. All the sleep up to this point was restless, my body and brain still adjusting. Thirty-six to forty-eight hours of poor sleep took its toll.

I'd rather be out longer, bypassing Tahiti to sail on off over the horizon, because it got better after the second night. But instead I poured a coffee, popped in a single headphone, and danced under the stars with not a soul to see me.

I took dance breaks whenever I needed to, singing along and moving my body, keeping myself awake. Standing behind the helm, I faced our wake and gyrated my hips to some AC/DC. I pistoned my pelvis, letting the boat rock under me and keeping my torso gimballing. On the beat, I hopped up, crossed my legs, and spun around to find a dark shape standing in front of me. I screamed.

"It is only me." Jonas laughed, bent over, while my heart raced in my chest.

"You're over an hour early! Holy shiitake!"

Jonas held out his arms and chased me around the helm while I tried to swat him away. He was still laughing, the bastard.

My harness got hooked on something and he caught me. The boat swayed and we dropped together onto the bench.

While the sunlight had disappeared hours ago, the moon was in full force, and up this close I could see Jonas's face clearly, the soft lines, the curve of his lips, and his long eyelashes.

"Sorry, Mia. I did not mean to startle you. I fell asleep so early that I woke up a little while ago and could not go back to sleep."

I turned slightly to face him. "And what am I supposed to do with all this adrenaline, huh? You scared the pants off me. I'll be awake for hours now."

He tweaked my nose. "Sorry. What can we do to put you to sleep?"

I sat up and stretched my back, twisting and turning, popping my spine. "Nothing, I'll stay up for a little while until I feel like sleeping again. We get in tomorrow; it's not a big deal."

"Does your back hurt?"

I rolled my neck. "I get stiff from sitting up here and hunching over my book. I had some better pillows out here, but they got moldy while the boat was stored in Apataki. I need to go shopping."

Jonas put a strong hand on my neck and rubbed the muscles on both sides of my spine. I rolled my head forward, stretching the muscles while he kneaded. We were both silent for a few minutes.

I broke the quiet. "How were you so calm today?"

"With the leak?"

"Yes."

He shifted behind me. "These things will only be better with calmness and thought. There is no reason to panic."

"But that was *an emergency*. We were sinking. I can't get over how calm you were."

"The more important to stay calm."

We were quiet again, and Jonas added another hand, moving to rub his thumbs further under my harness. I could feel my body relaxing more, and I took some deep breaths, trying to feel heavy and tired so I could sleep.

"What was Liam like, when you had an emergency?"

Jonas's question took me off guard, and I didn't want to answer. I didn't answer for a moment, trying to gather my thoughts and figure out what to tell him. He didn't push me, at least metaphorically. His hands were awesome, though.

"There was a lot of yelling. Liam, well, he hated when things went wrong. And things were a lot worse when I made a mistake."

He gave my neck an extra squeeze. "We all make mistakes."

A wave of relief rushed through me that he didn't comment any more than that. He could have jumped to defend Liam, or he could have brushed it off, but instead he stayed quiet.

"Did he call you names?"

I sat up, only just realizing that I'd been slumped back against Jonas. I spun around to face him. "How did you know that?"

Jonas ran a hand through his hair, tugging it slightly and looking off into the distance. "I have watched all your videos, you know this?"

I nodded in the dark.

He hesitated. "There were a few times where I thought maybe he was joking, or maybe he was not." I swallowed thickly, my eyes wide. "And there was that time where you did a live video. Just once."

"You watched that?"

"Ja."

Jonas was talking about the one and only live session we did. It was supposed to be a Q and A about our refit, and our channel had just had a big surge in subscribers. We had had about five hundred people watch live. The fact that Jonas was one of them shouldn't have surprised me: it was a smaller community than you'd think, and when Liam and I separated, several people had referenced the video while theorizing about our split.

I'd had to take the video down immediately. People were too unpredictable—Liam was too unpredictable. Some troll had made a crude comment, and Liam had swiftly spiraled into name-calling and yelling. It was humiliating and the moment when I stopped reading comments. From that day on, Liam had pulled further away from the filming aspect of our life. That quickly led to resentment, since it was our best source of income.

I didn't know what to say to that, but Jonas pulled me back closer to him and thankfully dropped the subject.

We talked for hours. He told me about growing up with only Eivind and his mom, and I told him about my big, loud family. He spoke fondly of his brother, and I told him about all the family drama. I stayed up way past the end of my shift, but I didn't mind. I could sleep when we got to Tahiti.

Around two thirty, Jonas kissed my forehead and sent me downstairs. I didn't want to leave him.

I lay in bed, smiling, rethinking the entire day and running it through my head. My mind kept replaying my favorite parts of Jonas, and combined with the restlessness of being on a small boat for a few days, I was fidgeting too much to fall asleep.

It had been a while since I'd had this feeling, but I rolled over and dug through the drawer beside my bed. I used to do this every night on passage to help myself fall asleep; I found my bullet vibrator—the only sex toy I had on board—and lay facedown with it pressed between my legs, over my panties. I thought of Jonas's smile, the quick glimpse of his ass and cock that I saw today, and ground into the vibrations.

I came quickly and rolled over, sweaty and breathing hard, kicking my sheets away to feel the cool breeze of the fan on my skin. And that was how I fell asleep.

———

"MIA."

Gentle fingers stroked my face. I opened my eyes and blinked hard against the sunlight.

"I am sorry to wake you." Jonas's face came into focus next to me. He straightened while I yawned and stretched myself out over the covers.

"Is everything okay?" When I looked over at him,

his eyes darted to my face from elsewhere, and a blush was creeping up his neck.

Jonas looked exhausted, his hair coming out of his ponytail and his eyes red and deep. The corner of his mouth ticked up. "Everything is fine, except I am falling asleep on my watch. I am sorry—can we switch?" His eyes were on me, almost too much.

"Yeah, of course." I lay back on the bed and rubbed my eyes. "Give me a few minutes and I'll come up."

"Ja." I heard him pad out of the room, and I sat up and blinked hard, waiting for my eyes to wake up, until something snagged my attention. My hot-pink bullet vibe sitting on top of my cream-colored sheets.

EIGHTEEN

WHEN I TOOK MY COFFEE UPSTAIRS, I WISHED JONAS A good nap, barely able to meet his eyes. I'd tucked my toy away in its proper place, banished until I was well and truly alone. I could see Tahiti in the distance and by the time Jonas was awake again, we were approaching the pass for the reef. Jonas stood at the bow, watching for hazards as I navigated us into the reef, Tahiti's famous surf breaking waves on either side.

We made it in easily and motored past *Eik* on a mooring ball. Jonas watched as we passed by. No one came outside, and their dinghy was gone. To save some money, I was staying one night on a mooring ball outside the marina, and Jonas helped me secure *Welina*.

"We could inflate my dinghy and row you over to *Eik*?" I asked once we were settled in.

Jonas looked thoughtful and shook his head. "I will stay here with you."

"I have to pack," I warned.

"That is okay." He picked up his book and settled in to read.

I went below to the forward cabin and started the arduous task of digging out my luggage. I had a few duffel bags tightly packed away somewhere. They were the kind that folded into their own little pouches to make them easy to store.

Item after item of stuff came out of the lockers. Soon I was surrounded by piles of baggage, stuff that weighed me and *Welina* down.

About half of the things were just things, forgotten items or afterthoughts. But the rest crowded around me, pushing memories at me. Here was the tool I'd dropped on the salon floor that had dented the wood. This was a diesel filter Liam had bought that we'd fought over and then never installed in the engine room.

Tears of frustration pricked my eyes. I'd *fought* to get this boat, fought with Liam to keep all this crap for an inkling of a chance that I could stay sailing. I'd replaced my memories at Kauehi with happy ones, yet I still carried around all this weight?

Finally I found two duffel bags, all that I would need for my trip. I looked at the mess of things scattered around me and swallowed thickly.

That was a task for another day. For now, I had to put things back and focus on packing. I reached for the item to the right of my foot and hesitated.

It was a hammock, the two wooden ends wrapped in the macrame sling. I had bought the hammock dreaming of tying it up on deck and lazing about. It never happened. Liam had berated me for buying something so "useless." His premonition came true: I had never pulled it out for fear of irritating him.

Something made me leave it out this time. After placing the hammock on the bed, I put the rest of the items away and went to go pack.

———

Two hours later my bags were packed and I was nearly ready for my flight. I rooted around in a cabinet, digging out some items I'd bought as gifts for my family, and my eye caught on the hammock again.

I threw the trinkets in my bag and tucked the hammock under my arm. Climbing the stairs, I found Jonas in the shade, still reading.

"No sign of your crew?" I said.

"No."

"Looks like you are stuck with me."

He gave me a soft smile. "I like that."

I gestured to my hammock. "I am going to set this up. I've never actually used it."

"Do you want help?"

"Sure."

Jonas followed me out on the deck. The sun was declining, the air starting to cool. My intention was to set the hammock up with one end on my headsail and one end around the mast.

It took us a while to figure it out, but with a little ingenuity and knot-tying on Jonas's part, the hammock swung in the slight breeze.

I sat on the edge, testing the weight. I leaned more and more until I could swing my legs over, comfortably lounging.

I closed my eyes and laughed.

"Is it comfortable?"

I scrunched up my face. "To sleep, yes. But maybe to read I'd need a pillow."

"I will get you one." Jonas turned to walk back to the cockpit.

"Oh, wait! Get me my book too!" He flashed a smile over his shoulder. "And your book!"

This time he turned around and looked at me. "My book?"

"Yeah. It's a two-person hammock." I gestured next to me.

The smile Jonas gave me was blinding. He disappeared out of view and returned a few minutes later, practically giddy. It took a bit to get him situated; we giggled as the hammock pitched up when Jonas sat on the edge, and when he swung his legs over we both tumbled together in the middle and I laughed so hard, I cried.

Finally we were settled next to each other. The press of Jonas's warm skin against me was comforting. He kept a leg dangling off the side, gently pushing us back and forth, occasionally slowing us when the boat rocked too hard in the small waves around us.

I read until I got drowsy, closing my eyes and allowing the book to collapse on my chest.

I BLINKED AWAKE, DISORIENTED FOR A MOMENT. WHERE was I? It was dark, but a gentle breeze wafted over me.

Warm skin was under my cheek, a heavy arm pressed around me. I swallowed and shifted.

"Mia?" Jonas whispered.

"Hey. I fell asleep on you?"

"Ja."

"Sorry."

"It is okay."

"What time is it?"

"I do not know. Late."

"Oh, Jonas, I am so sorry." I struggled to sit up, rocking the hammock lightly. "It's after dinner—your crew is probably back by now."

Jonas's hand ran along my spine. "It is okay," he repeated. "You slept hard, ja?"

I wiped the back of my hand over my mouth. "Yeah. Let's go eat something."

We climbed out of the hammock and made our way into the cockpit. I caught sight of the clock by the navigation desk.

"Ten o'clock! Oh my God! Jonas, try hailing your boat, see if they will come get you."

He tried to hail his brother while I dished out the last of the pasta salad. I opened a tin of tuna and mixed it in.

Jonas had gotten no response from *Eik*. He turned to me and shrugged. "What do you want to do?"

I hesitated. "Well, we could get my dinghy down and I could drive you over to *Eik*, or you could stay here."

He swallowed, Adam's apple bobbing. "Where would you like me to sleep?"

We stared at each other. The thought of Jonas in my bed the past few nights had been almost torturous. I knew in my heart that we should keep a safe distance. I was leaving tomorrow, I might never see him again, and at this point I was too invested. I didn't think I could handle anything physical.

But damned if I didn't want those memories.

"You can sleep in my bed with me. It's big enough. And it already smells like you."

Jonas smiled broadly. "It smells like me?"

"Well, yeah. It's good. I mean . . . you smell nice." I shoved a bowl of pasta salad in his hands to stop my babbling. "Here. Dinner."

I sat at the table and Jonas followed me. We ate in silence, but I stole glances at him. His hair was a mess, with sections lumping up out of his ponytail, and he, too, had sleep lines on his face.

"We may not fall asleep for a while since we both took a nap."

"True. We can read for a little longer if you would like."

I nodded. "I think I have some herbal tea somewhere too."

"Good."

Jonas washed the dishes while I dug out some

chamomile tea. In the tight quarters of my galley, I worked at pulling the collapsible kettle out of the cabinet. I nudged Jonas aside to fill it with water and he waited patiently, sudsy hands hovering over the sink.

When I faced the stove, we were back-to-back. Our butts brushed together occasionally, and I could feel his warmth through my clothes, making me think about how I'd woken up in the hammock, pressed against him.

When the mugs were put out and the kettle had started heating up, I stepped out of the way. The sink faced the bow of the boat, and directly in front of the sink was one side of the couch. I kneeled on the cushions, facing Jonas, resting my butt on the table and my hands on the short wall at the back of the couch.

I was waiting for the kettle to boil. No sense in picking up my book when I'd need to turn off the stove in a few minutes.

Jonas looked up from his washing occasionally, eyes twinkling while I watched him work. He had these long slender fingers with neatly trimmed nails. He was quick and efficient at the dishes.

"Do you wash the dishes a lot on your boat?"

He smiled. "No, usually I am excused from that duty since we have so many people on board."

I nodded. "There are a lot more important things to be done around the boat."

He hummed and the kettle behind him whistled. I scooted around him and poured the hot water into the mugs.

Jonas brushed against me, turning around in the small galley and resting his palms on the counter on either side of me, gently caging me in.

"Where do you want to drink your tea?" I could feel his breath against my hair.

I cleared my throat. "Upstairs?"

He took a hand off the counter and grabbed my waist, squeezing lightly before he picked up one of the mugs and carried it to the cockpit.

I followed behind him and paused at the top of the stairs. We were so . . . domestic. Last night had been different, having to keep watch and sleep in shifts, but this felt like the start of a routine. A comfortable routine.

Jonas blew on his tea to cool it, picked up his book, and focused his attention on the pages. I hemmed and hawed for a moment about where to sit. I wanted to sit next to Jonas.

It struck me suddenly and I blurted out my thoughts. "When will I see you again?"

He looked at me. "What do you mean?" He blew on his tea again and took a testing sip.

"I leave tomorrow, and I'll be back in two weeks. But where will you be when I come back?" I shifted my weight. "Don't you need to move on?"

Jonas propped his arm up on the backrest next to him and gestured me in. I sat down next to him, close enough to feel his warmth, and he curled his arm around me. He leaned in, resting his cheek on my hair. "I would like to be here when you get back."

I gripped my mug tightly. "Yeah?" A grin spread on my lips.

"Ja."

Things could change, and I knew how the cruising life was. Even if Jonas wanted to be here when I got back, something might come up and *Eik* would have to go. My heart panged at the thought that even the best laid plans could go astray, especially in sailing, and tomorrow could be the last time I'd see Jonas—ever. Friends were constantly going in and out of my life, and Jonas—and the rest of the *Eik* crew—would be a shame to lose. Perhaps I was more tangled up, invested, and emotional since these were my first real friendships since my divorce.

That must be what it was.

NINETEEN

THE TEA WORKED BETTER THAN I EXPECTED, AND combined with the warmth and comfort of Jonas next to me, I quickly became drowsy. Jonas nudged me awake and we went downstairs to get ready for bed.

I took the head first, and when I came out, Jonas was sitting on the bed, still dressed and waiting. We swapped, and I stripped. Usually I would sleep nude, especially with the heat, but . . .

Full-on pajamas seemed too prude—and also, hot.

I wondered what Jonas was going to wear to bed, and then realized he was probably waiting for a cue from me. I sighed and then dressed in cotton underwear and a tank top, crawling onto the bed.

I was facing away when Jonas came out, giving him privacy as he changed for bed. The mattress depressed under his weight; the light by his side of the bed clicked off.

I heard Jonas sigh deeply. "Good night, Mia."

"Good night," I whispered.

We lay in bed together, the boat rocking us and cool air blowing against our bodies with every rotation of the fan. I'd had so many thoughts about possibilities with Jonas in bed with me, but they quickly faded to black, my mind and body too tired.

———

I WOKE UP WITH A SMOOTH EXPANSE OF SKIN DIRECTLY IN front of me. I was warm—so warm—and groggier than usual.

My cheek was pressed against Jonas's chest, my arm wrapped around him, and our legs intertwined. I looked up and found Jonas above me, smiling while he watched me wake up.

"Good morning."

"Morning." I pulled back as Jonas rearranged his arms. When he moved his arm out from behind me, I could see that he had a book in his hand and had been reading.

I yawned and stretched out, my shoulders cracking and my tank top riding up my stomach. When I opened my eyes again, Jonas was lying on his stomach, propped up on his arms and watching me. He was wearing black briefs, his legs bare against my sheets. Most Americans wore boxer-style underwear, not this European fashion. I wanted to reach out and trace my fingers over the edge, where his thigh disappeared, but I resisted with Herculean effort.

"What time is it?"

Jonas rolled his wrist and checked his watch. "Seven."

I hummed and rolled to my side, facing him. "Later than normal, but not too bad."

Jonas put his book aside and then reached a hand out to my face. He hesitated, and then slid his fingers into my hair, smoothing it back. I closed my eyes and let him caress me.

Until there was a knocking on the side of the boat.

"Jonas? Mia?" I heard a voice call out.

Jonas and I grinned at each other and climbed out of bed. "Coming!" I called through the open hatch.

We both pulled on shorts and climbed up top.

"Good morning, Eivind. Would you like to come up?"

"Good morning, Mia! Yes, please." Eivind tied his dinghy to *Welina* and climbed aboard. "How was your sail over?"

"A little eventful." I told him about my thru-hull problem as we walked into the salon. Jonas had started a pot of coffee, and began to add tidbits to my story.

When we finished, Eivind told us about their passage, which had been easy. No near sinkings on *Eik*.

Eivind declined a cup of coffee. "We were going to head into Carrefour today. Marcella is excited to reprovision. Do you want to come with us?"

I shook my head. "I will have to shop when I get back. For now, I have enough to last until I leave."

"Jonas?"

"I will stay and help Mia get *Welina* into the marina."

"Ah yes, that will be much easier, thank you." Docking boats was the hardest part, and usually the most embarrassing. I was an expert, but even still, it would be good to have a linehandler on board.

"Okay, we will go, then." Eivind tapped his fist on the table, but made no move to get up. "We spent some time yesterday using the internet at the marina."

Jonas nodded.

"Marcella has a phone interview next week."

I looked between Jonas and Eivind. "That's good, yes?"

Jonas smiled sadly. "Good for her but bad for us." His lips turned down and he rubbed his brow.

"She wanted me to talk to you about it before she made any moves. Make sure we will be okay. Are we going to look for another crew member?" Eivind asked.

Sighing, Jonas leaned back on the couch. "What do you think?"

I felt a little uncomfortable having this discussed in front of me, but I would guess that Jonas and Eivind didn't have much alone time on the boat without the crew around.

"Lila does not like the sailing much either, but she is learning."

"And she will not leave you." Jonas smiled at his brother and teased him. "Just do not do anything stupid."

"She said yes. I think I am doing good."

"Anyway," Jonas continued, "I do not think we need another crew member. It was our intention to only have four of us on board anyway."

Eivind darted his eyes over to me. "That is, if Elayna stays."

"Right. If Elayna stays."

A pang of jealousy hit me. I knew that Jonas was spending so much time with me, but long-term? Elayna was going to be there, for as long as she wanted, it seemed.

"Okay." Eivind stood up. "Have fun moving the boat. We will return with lots of food!"

We waved goodbye to Eivind and I hailed the marina on the VHF to get directions and make sure my dock was free. Jonas prepared breakfast and we ate quickly before pulling out fenders and lines, firing up the engine and heading toward the marina.

The winds were calm; I didn't have to worry about the current. But even with tranquil conditions, my heart beat a little faster and my palms got sticky.

Jonas stood at the port side of the boat, holding on to the rigging and standing at the ready to handle lines.

I motored *Welina* past the fuel dock and squinted at the numbers on the dock, trying to find my slip. When I found the right aisle, I turned the wheel, sending *Welina* into a ninety-degree turn down the aisle.

My fingers were tense, and I tried to open and close my hand and take some deep breaths. It was going to be a heck of a lot easier to do this if I could get it on the first try. If I missed the slip, I would have to come all the way out and approach it again. No matter how many times you docked your boat, it was still a pain in the ass.

And of course, anytime a boat came into a slip, people had to stop and watch. And in this case, it was even worse: the rest of the *Eik* crew was walking the dock and scoping out the marina before going grocery shopping. They stopped and put down their bags, preparing to catch lines.

I felt my heartbeats, counting them until the right moment when I spun the helm and *Welina*'s bow veered toward the slip. I corrected course early, shifted into neutral, and let *Welina* glide into the slip. Jonas tossed the spring line to Eivind on the dock, and I gently shifted into reverse. With the engine and Eivind securing the line, *Welina* came to a halt perfectly in her slip.

Jonas played deckhand and followed my instructions, working to get the lines just right. When I finished checking and tightening the lines, I stepped back and surveyed my boat.

Beside me, Jonas slipped an arm around my shoulders. "You did good."

I smiled, finally. "Yeah, I did."

Lila bounced on her toes on the dock. "Forget free-diving lessons. Mia, teach me how to *drive* like that!"

Jonas squeezed me close to him.

TWENTY

IN THE MARINA OFFICE, I FILLED OUT MULTIPLE PAGES OF paperwork for my slip. The receptionist looked them over, then pointed to a blank section I hadn't filled out. "You are leaving the boat here and exiting the country, yes?"

I nodded.

"Who is your caretaker?"

"Caretaker?"

"Yes, you need someone to be held responsible while you are gone, in case anything happens or your boat has a problem."

"Uh—"

"I will be the caretaker," Jonas interrupted. He was sitting in one of the upholstered chairs, flipping through a magazine.

"Really? Are you sure?"

"Yes, of course. We will be here anyway."

I looked at him skeptically. "Your plans could change."

"Nah."

"Okay." I handed the form over and Jonas wrote down his name and number. The receptionist helped me arrange a taxi to the airport for my flight. Jonas and I walked back to the boat and I showed him where I was going to leave a spare key, just in case.

I checked the time. "My taxi will pick me up in a little bit. I have to finish packing."

Jonas read while I gathered my things and dragged them to the cockpit. He helped me unload them onto the dock.

"Why don't you stay on the boat until your crew comes back from the supermarket?"

"Thank you. I will, but let me help you with the bags." He threw a duffel over his shoulder, and I hefted up the other one. As we walked down the dock, Jonas rested his hand on my lower back.

It hit me suddenly—I was going back home. While I was excited to see my family, I was also going to miss Jonas, this companion whom I'd had for the last month. We'd spent so much time together now; how would I be able to quit him cold turkey?

While he said they would be here the whole time I was gone, sailing plans were written in the sand at low tide. Things could change, and it was very possible that Jonas and the rest of *Eik* would be gone by the time I got back.

That was part of the lifestyle, but that didn't give me any comfort. Cruising friends often came and went in my life, but Jonas . . . I wanted Jonas to stay. But part of me knew that this wasn't in the cards for us. Our futures were too different. Jonas had an end goal and a home to return to thousands of miles away from mine. He had made a commitment to his brother, who'd changed his whole life to help Jonas accomplish his dream. He had to see it all the way through, even if it meant leaving me behind.

———

THE TAXI WAITED FOR ME AT THE CURB. THE DRIVER popped the trunk, and we arranged my bags in the back.

Jonas opened the car door for me.

I started to say I'd stay in touch when I had a realization. "Jonas, I don't have any of your contact info!" The thought was terrifying: I was going to leave my boat—my home and all my worldly possessions—with someone I couldn't even get a message to, and only a few minutes ago I was thinking how much I wanted him to stay in my life.

Jonas was unruffled, though, and smiled. "Give me your phone."

I dug my phone out of my purse and unlocked it before handing it to him. Jonas added his contact information and sent himself a message. "There. Now you will be able to talk to me." He handed back the phone. "I promise I will take good care of your girl."

"Thank you."

Jonas opened his mouth but then hesitated. I waited for him to speak, but instead he caught me by surprise. His hand cupped my cheek, his fingers sliding into my hair and his thumb tilting my chin up. Gently, Jonas bent and brushed his lips against mine.

I breathed him in for a moment, my stomach flipping over and my heart pounding. When I didn't move, he kissed me again, pressing our lips firmly together.

He pulled back slightly, shifting his weight and stepping away, but he allowed his lips to linger one moment more. Before he could pull away completely, I gripped his shirt and tugged him toward to me.

With that permission, we swept together. I slid an arm behind his back, pressing us closer. His fingers tightened, gripping my hair harder, squeezing every time his tongue swept my mouth. I took huge, gulping breaths of him until I was dizzy and achy and felt like I'd burst out of my skin.

We broke apart, both wide-eyed and breathing hard. Slowly, Jonas grinned at me and, untangling his fingers from my hair, touched the tip of my nose gently with his finger.

"See you soon," he whispered softly.

I nodded, a little lost without him pressing against me. Jonas gently touched my back with his hand, guiding me down into the car. The door shut, the taxi drove away, and my brain tried to pull me back to reality.

With my fingertips, I traced my lips, which were plump and sensitive. The taste of Jonas lingered. I closed my eyes and smiled.

TWENTY-ONE

At the airport I waited until I reached the gate to pull out my phone. I had a message from Jonas. It was careful and neutral. *Have a good flight.* I could picture Jonas assessing me, testing the waters.

No way.

That was some kiss, I messaged back.

Immediately my phone pinged.

Thank God. Best kiss of my life.

I laughed and crossed my legs, settling into my chair. Another message pinged in.

Are you at the gate?

Yes. Where are you?

In your bed. Too creepy?

My stomach fluttered. This new Jonas, this Jonas who kissed me senseless, was in my bed. I could picture it, his tanned skin and blond hair splayed on my sheets.

You make me want to miss my flight.

I will be here when you get back. If that is what you want.

Yes, please.

I cannot wait. I miss you already. Eivind is here now. I have to go.

Talk soon.

———

MY FLIGHTS WERE UNEVENTFUL: SEVEN HOURS TO LOS Angeles, and three to Seattle. When my plane landed in LA, I had a message waiting for me from Jonas, hoping I had had a good flight and wishing me a good night. I sighed, knowing that our time apart would be challenging with different time zones.

I shielded my eyes from the bright sunrise when I stepped out of the Sea-Tac, looking for James, who had volunteered to pick me up. Finally I spotted him in the crowd.

"Hey, Miamati!"

James and I embraced.

"Sir James." I nodded at him regally and we both grinned. His smile dropped quickly, though.

"You don't look so good."

"Gee, thanks, little brother."

He cocked a look at me. "You know what I mean. You've lost weight and look a little haggard. Mom's gonna kill you." *Leave it to my brother to be blunt.*

"Well, usually it's a food fest when I come home anyway. I doubt this time will be any different."

James flung one of my bags over his shoulder and we walked out to the car while he asked all the pleasantries. Yes, my flight was good; no, I wasn't hungry; yes, I wanted to drive straight to my parents' house.

James still lived here in Seattle too, but he had his own place out in Ballard. I would stay with him instead of with my parents, since my out-of-town siblings and their families were flying in too. Between the three siblings in Seattle and my parents' place, no one was staying in a hotel, though the families were being split up. My niblings were given choices: they could stay wherever their parents were, or they could go "camping" in the basement of my parents' house.

That explained the ruckus that greeted us when we walked into Mom and Dad's place. With six grandchildren sleeping in the basement, my parents were in seventh heaven. When my mom opened the door to greet us, though, she was harried.

"Mia's here to help me chase down every single one of you!" she bellowed to the stampede behind her. She hugged me quickly. "Come on in. Your father is over at Ike's house, helping to inspect the fence. He'll be back after dinner."

The youngest kids squealed and turned tail, running back into the depths of the house. One of my older nephews, Tyrell, passed by with headphones in and nodded. "S'up."

Welcome to the pandemonium.

———

MUCH, MUCH LATER, WHEN THE KIDS WERE TUCKED into their sleeping bags and watching movies downstairs with James supervising, I finally got a calm and proper greeting from my mom. She hugged me tightly and guided me to the kitchen table.

"How are things back on *Welina*?" She brushed my hair back from my face. "You don't look so good."

"James already gave me a heckling. I'm fine. A few problems came up on the sail over to Tahiti, but I'll tackle them when I get back."

"Well, I am so glad you were near an airport and able to fly back home to see us. The service will be so lovely and your grandmother would be so proud to have all of her grandchildren and great-grandchildren here." Mom squeezed my hand. "Thank you for coming back."

"I'm glad to be here. I haven't seen Dawn or Hunter in ages. Our visits have never seemed to overlap."

We picked at the remaining pizza in the boxes; we had been too busy earlier to eat anything while my horde of niblings ate. Mom filled me in on each of my siblings. I was closest to James and Dawn, but also to Doug's wife, Miranda, who was always keeping me in the loop via email.

Mom and I cleaned up, and it was dark out when my dad's car pulled into the driveway. He barreled into the house, slamming the garage door behind him. "Mia!"

"Hush, Larry. The kids are downstairs watching a movie and I bet some of them are asleep."

"Shh, shh, shh," Dad teased, while tiptoeing over to give me a hug. "Patty, that son of yours is handier than pockets on a shirt. He got that fence installed and it looks fantastic." He kissed Mom's cheek and grabbed a slice of pizza. I smiled, thinking of Jonas's gentle kisses. "And how's our Miamati doing?"

"Everything's fine, Dad."

Dad ruffled my hair. "Are things on the boat better now that Liam's out?"

"Yes. They are definitely better."

"What about your sailing friends?" Mom asked me.

"Most of them have moved on already. There are so few boats in that part of the world, and for sure not many stay very long. Most boats still have a long way to go to get to safety for cyclone season."

Mom clucked. "I worry about you all alone."

"But now the boat's in Tahiti. There are lots of boats in Tahiti."

"True."

My phone dinged in my backpack and I was sure it was Jonas, checking to see if I got in okay. "Hang on," I told my parents.

Sure enough, it was Jonas asking if I was home safe. I typed a quick reply and smiled when I saw a picture he sent me: *Eik* had moved into the marina too and was right next to *Welina*.

Now I will be able to keep a close eye on her for you. And I'll have Wi-Fi more often to talk to you.

I looked up to find my parents both watching me. Mom smiled, all saccharine. "Who's that?"

I turned the screen off and stuffed the phone into my pocket. "The caretaker who's looking after *Welina*."

She nodded and took a sip from her wine. "How did you find them?"

"He's on another cruising boat."

"But I thought you didn't have any friends in the area?"

I rolled my eyes. "Mom, okay, fine, I have a friend."

"What's his name?"

"Jonas."

"Is he single?"

"Mom! Seriously, you have four children popping out grandbabies for you, and three of your children are happily married."

She sniffed. "That's only a fifty-percent success rate. And it's not the grandbabies I'm really after; I just want you to be happy."

I gentled my tone. "Thanks, Mom."

"Are you going to be happy on the boat? By yourself—"

Dad interrupted. "Of course she'll be happy. She's my little sailor girl." He ruffled my hair again and stood up. "Now, ladies, I'm tired. I'm going to bed. Mia, you better come around a lot while you are here. Gotta make up for not staying with us." He squeezed me really hard, squishing the breath out of my lungs.

"It's not my fault Dawn and her brood claimed the guest rooms first."

Dad waved me off and headed upstairs.

My sister had three kids: the oldest grandchild, who had a room to himself, as a teenager should, and two younger ones, who were downstairs watching the Disney movie.

"Where is Dawn anyway?"

"She and Marvin went to catch up with friends tonight. Take advantage of the free babysitting."

"That's fair."

Mom caught me up on the kids, detailing the activities they all partook in. With my three siblings who still lived in the Seattle area, Mom was pretty involved in her grandma status, driving kids around and dropping by to help around the house. She knew *everything*.

"Speak of the devil."

James was at the top of the stairs that led to the basement, blinking in the harsher light of the kitchen.

"Those kids . . . energy . . . need beer." He mock staggered around the kitchen, pulling a beer out of the fridge and grabbing a cookie from the cookie jar —yes, my mom literally kept a cookie jar on the counter.

"Is everyone asleep?" Mom asked.

"Near enough." He sighed and slipped into the chair next to me at the table. "Lee is reading and Aaron is playing with his handheld gaming thingy. But they are both in their sleeping bags."

"Look at you," I teased him. "Such a good uncle."

"Damn right I am."

"Well, I am sorry I have no beds to offer you for the night. You'll have to go home," Mom said to James.

"I know, Mom." Mom hated that they had down-sized when James was in high school, but it made sense, even if the whole family couldn't get together in one house anymore.

When James finished his beer, Mom shooed us out of the house. James tossed me the keys and then climbed into the passenger seat and navigated me to his house.

Once in his guest bedroom, I kicked off my shoes and lay on the bed.

You there? I messaged Jonas.

For you, always.

What did you do today, other than move Eik?

We went to Carrefour again.

Haha, really? I bet Marcella is loving it.

Yes, but it is bittersweet. She has a beautiful market to shop in, but our budget for food is nothing compared to what she normally works with.

That would be hard. A chef with her skills can make anything delicious, though.

True. How is your family?

Good. I only saw my parents and niblings today. And James, of course.

Do you miss the boat already?

No, not yet.

I hesitated before sending the next message.

I do miss you, though.

I miss you too. What did you do tonight?

We had pizza and movie night, which was good. Less effort from us adults and I am too exhausted for the kind of running around my mom likes to do.

I bet your parents are happy to have you back. Are you staying with them?

No, I'm at James's. It's only about twenty minutes away, something James complains about all the time.

I bet. It is pretty late over there. Do I need to make you go to sleep?

Boo. I'd rather talk to you.

I will be here tomorrow. Go to sleep.

Fiiiiine. Night.

Night.

TWENTY-TWO

IN THE MORNING, JAMES SAID HE HAD TO GO TO THE grocery store, and I jumped at the chance to go with him.

"Do you know how long it's been since I've been to a real, proper grocery store?"

James grunted as we pulled into the parking lot.

"Three months, James. Three months of picking through older, imported vegetables. Three months of spearfishing. Three months of figuring out when the supply ship would come so I could get first dibs on stuff."

Inside, I was like a kid in a candy store. "Look at these beautiful strawberries. I can't get these in Polynesia. And look at these beets; they would keep forever on the boat."

My eyes grew big when I spotted rows and rows of chocolate bars.

In the meantime, James was grumbling on every aisle.

"They don't have the kombucha I like. Where are the organic eggs? They have free-range, grass-fed, and cage-free, but where are the Goddamn organic ones?"

I couldn't help snarking at him. "I think all the eggs in Kauehi are organic."

James sighed and rolled his eyes at me.

I added another item into the cart and James eyed the massive pile of groceries accumulating. "Why are you shopping so much? Am I paying for your groceries? We're eating with the family every day."

I picked up a jar of peanut butter and hugged it to my chest. "This one is coming back to the boat with me."

"You have organic eggs but not peanut butter?"

"Well, maybe they do. I haven't been to the store yet in Tahiti. But yeah, usually these islands don't have peanut butter. And when they do, it's in the international section."

"Heaven forbid you go without a peanut butter and honey sandwich."

"Oh! Sandwich bread."

"I have some at home."

"You have gluten-free sliced cardboard is what you have."

Several aisles later, I was dillydallying, picking things up and putting them down in the candy aisle. I wondered what I could bring back to Tahiti with me, something that Jonas would like, something that would be a treat. My mind was completely blank. How much time had I spent with him over the past few weeks, and why was it so hard to think of something to bring him?

Did I really know him at all?

"What are you doing?" James interrupted my thoughts.

"Nothing." I sighed.

"You were mooning over more 'American' stuff, weren't you?" He made a face at me. "What's missing from your life in Tahiti again?"

We spent the rest of the trip bickering at each other until we were loading the car and James's phone rang.

"It's Mom," he said. "Hello? Yeah, she's here with me." James pressed the phone to his chest. "Mom wants to know why you aren't answering your phone."

I frowned. "I don't have my phone with me."

"Mom, Mia doesn't have her phone with her." Before he'd even gotten a response from Mom, he tilted the phone down. "Why don't you have your phone with you?"

"Because I don't have service here unless I'm on Wi-Fi."

"She says she doesn't— You know what, Mom? You talk to her." James handed me the phone.

"Hi, Mom. I don't have any cell phone service here. You can only reach me when I have Wi-Fi."

"Aren't you going to buy a SIM card?" she asked. "You should have a phone to use."

"Mom, I'm going to be here for less than two weeks and I don't even have a car. I'll probably be right with James every single second." I ignored James's sarcastic "yay" as we climbed into the car.

It took the entire drive back to James's place to convince Mom that I would be fine and she didn't need to buy me a SIM card or a burner phone. I assured her that James and I would be over before lunch.

When I hung up, James was unloading the car.

"You got in *troubleee*."

———

LUNCH WAS A LOUD ORDEAL. WHEN WE ARRIVED AT noon, the meal was in full swing.

Dawn and her family were there, and Hunter and

his two teenagers, who were staying at Doug's house, were there too, so we had eight adults, three teenagers, and six children. Most of the younger kids and my mom were seated around the table, the kitchen a smorgasbord of sandwich fixings. The rest of the family was at the dining room table.

I called out a hello to all my niblings and gave them hugs. The oldest granddaughter, Erica, wrapped her arms around me and tilted her face up to mine.

"Dad says you've been to Tahiti. Is that true?"

Hunter, her dad and my brother, chimed in. "She's obsessed with surfing right now."

"Yes, my boat's in Tahiti."

Her eyes widened. "How does your boat not get hit with all those big waves?"

"Well, the big waves are on the other side of the island, I think. Or maybe out at the barrier reef. I'm not sure. Plus, there's also a season for big waves."

"What season do they get the big waves in Tahiti?"

"I'm not sure about that either."

"Erica, stop bothering Aunt Mia. Eat your lunch."

I made a sandwich and sat down next to my dad.

"Patty, did you turn the air-conditioning off? It's hotter than a hooker in a cucumber patch in here."

"Dad!" Hunter covered Erica's ears. "You can't talk about hookers at the table!"

"Erica knows what hookers are."

"Yeah, I know what hookers are."

"I don't care!" Hunter hissed. "We don't talk about hookers at the table."

Dad smirked at me. "As I was saying, did you turn the air-conditioning off, Patty? It's hotter than a prostitute in a cucumber patch."

James actually snorted soda up his nose and Hunter scolded my dad some more. He acted repentant, but I knew he would only get worse as Hunter's visit went on. While the rest of us had stopped cursing or replaced our curse words around the niblings, Dad loved to rile his kids, especially Hunter.

With so many people around, the conversation flowed and spiraled. There were never dull moments with my family, and I thought back over the last few months: the quiet diligence in the boatyard, the absolute solitude of cruising the Tuamotus. Some people might be attracted to silence after a loud upbringing, but that wasn't me. I loved sailing despite the fact that it was a quiet activity, not because of it.

"Hey, Mia," Dawn's husband, Marvin, said, pulling me back to the conversation. "I watched a documentary the other day about this woman who sailed solo around the world."

"Oh yeah? Which documentary?"

"I don't remember the name of it, but she was sailing, like, nonstop?"

Ronnie, Dawn's middle child, piped up. "Just like Mia!"

"Well, no," I said. "I don't sail nonstop."

"Why not?"

I laughed. "Okay, how long do you think it would take to sail around the world?"

Ronnie looked at the ceiling, kicking his legs under the table.

"Umm." He bit his lip, and maybe it was because I hadn't seen him in a few years, but it struck me suddenly how much he looked like his mom. "Three weeks?"

I widened my eyes. "Longer."

He grinned at me. "Four weeks?"

I laughed and inched my finger toward his ribs. He giggled at the mere thought of being tickled, but then straightened up. "No, Aunt Mia."

I put my finger away. "Longer than four weeks."

"How long?"

I crinkled my eyes and thought. "It would probably take me seven or eight months."

Ronnie's eyes widened, and he looked at his dad for confirmation.

"I'd need a different boat, though, and a support team, and a lot of planning. It's probably not the right time of year to start that kind of trip now."

Across the table, Erica, who'd been listening, spoke up. "But you *could* do it, right?"

I looked at my plate instead of meeting her eyes. A memory popped into my head of Hunter telling me that Erica wanted to come help me and "star" in my videos, even when we were in the hot boatyard, working on filthy projects and filming honest videos about how much things sucked. Hunter had been a little annoyed at me when I sent her a copy of Laura Dekker's autobiography for Christmas.

"Of course I could."

TWENTY-THREE

James and I got home from my parents' house at a reasonable hour that night, and I messaged Jonas, crossing my fingers and hoping he wasn't out at dinner or busy with his crew.

He answered by calling me with a video chat. I did the stupid thing where I fluffed my hair and checked my teeth before answering. When the call connected, I saw Jonas sitting in his bed, his hair pulled back and his face deeply shadowed by the harsh light.

"Hey, you're in bed."

"So are you. You had a good time with your family today?"

I filled him in on my day: shopping with James and spending the afternoon with Dawn and her family at Pike Place Market.

"What have you guys been doing today?"

"We went to the *roulottes* in town here."

I shook my head at him. "I don't know what that is."

"In downtown Papeete, there are . . . I forget the English word." He pinched the bridge of his nose. "They are vans, and they serve food. . . ."

"Oh, food trucks."

"Yes, food trucks. Not vans." He laughed at himself. "When you come back, I will take you out to dinner at the roulottes. You like poisson cru?"

"I love it." The national dish, poisson cru, was served all over the islands: freshly caught fish soaked in lime juice and coconut milk. "Was it pretty good tonight?"

Jonas slipped down on the bed, lying on his side and propping his head up on his hand. "Very good. Fresh and cheap."

"How's *Welina*?"

"Good. It is too dark outside, or else I would show you, but she is happy to be next door to us."

"What else have you been up to, other than the roulottes?"

Jonas gave me a look. "Mia, we have been bad."

"How so?"

"We sat all day and used the internet. We did nothing else."

I groaned and rolled my face into my pillow. "I *know*. I was absolutely glued to my phone in LAX. Having fast Wi-Fi is like a drug." I peeked at him. "Were you actually working?"

He wiggled his head. "Sometimes yes, sometimes no." He slid down even further, lying flat on his side, and I did the same. "Marcella has an interview this week," he reminded me.

"Oh yeah. I would guess Tahiti would be a pretty easy place to leave *Eik*, right? Marcella can fly almost anywhere."

"Ja."

Jonas was silent for a moment, thinking.

"Are you happy or sad about it?" I asked him.

"I think . . . I am more sad. Marcella was a special catch for us. She is professional, and really easygoing. And I am worried about how our crew will do without her."

"I'm sorry."

"Thank you." Jonas yawned. He shifted, getting more comfortable on the bed. "There is one other thing I have been doing."

I raised an eyebrow and Jonas grinned sheepishly.

"I am always thinking about that kiss."

A flush spread from my chest across my body. "I think about it too."

His smile widened. "Ja?"

"Of course." I rolled my eyes, a little uncomfortable with his enthusiasm, my feelings, and a little bit of nasty emotion in the pit of my stomach that I couldn't name.

"Mia," he said gently. "It has been a long time since Liam, ja?"

"Yeah."

He settled onto his side, resting his head in the crook of his arm. "Can we talk about him?"

My heart rate picked up and my stomach felt a little queasy. "What do you want to know?"

Jonas looked off camera and ran his fingers through his hair. "How bad did it get?"

"He didn't hit me if that's what you're asking."

Jonas audibly exhaled. "Okay."

We were both quiet, and I picked at the sheets underneath me. Jonas watched me. "Our relationship didn't start out bad. I mean, relationships never do, right?"

"Relationships are complicated, and my marriage may not have been happy, but I do not believe it was ever *bad* for me." His voice turned soft. "But I also don't know anyone else who was in a really bad relationship."

When I wasn't forthcoming, Jonas flipped the topic. "Tell me some good things."

I told Jonas how Liam and I had met, how we'd

dated and married and struggled through jobs and family issues before buying *Welina*. Talking about the good stuff had loosened me up. "Us moving aboard *Welina* was kind of a role reversal. Yes, Liam liked sailing and was learning a lot really quickly, but he was never going to have it in his blood like I do."

"Salt water in your veins."

"Yeah, exactly. I think he started to resent it. He was the boss before we bought the boat—at work and at home—and it chipped away at him."

I flipped to my stomach, propping up on my elbows, the phone resting on the pillows. "What about your ex-wife?"

"She was never a sailor. I took her out a few times, but she did not enjoy it. I had never vocalized my sailing dreams, so I left them by the side."

"She wasn't a sailor? How did you meet, then?"

"At a work event. It was . . . networking? Where you meet with people in similar jobs or industries?"

"Yeah, networking." I smiled a little bit, having a hard time picturing Jonas as anything other than a sailor. "Did you wear a suit and tie to work?"

He chuckled. "Ja."

I hummed, picturing it. "Did you have your long hair back then?"

Jonas beamed. "You like the long hair?"

"Mm-hmm."

"Well, no, I did not. That is a new thing. Anyway, I met Anika at a networking event. I asked her for drinks afterward, and then we dated." He waved a hand. "It was a very normal relationship. Until it wasn't."

We were both quiet, lost in our own thoughts for a few minutes.

"Let's get some sleep, okay?" I yawned. "We can talk tomorrow."

Jonas turned to look at me. "Tomorrow," he agreed.

I smiled, attempting to imprint on my brain this one last view of Jonas before I hung up. "Night."

———

I HAD BROUGHT MY LAPTOP WITH ME AND THE SD cards from my cameras, so the next morning at James's house, when I couldn't sleep, I worked on making a video. I set up in the breakfast nook just off the kitchen, and as daylight brightened the room around me.

While I hadn't planned anything out, I had some miscellaneous footage: snorkeling, a few shots of *Welina* sailing, and the drone footage.

I didn't have many clips of me talking to the camera, but when I did, it was like a different person from the footage a few weeks prior. I had better color, my smile actually reached my eyes, I looked more relaxed.

Excited, I reviewed all the footage, slid the best clips into the software program, and found a song to work with. The trickiest part was the sunset time-lapse I'd done at the beach, but I managed to get a halfway presentable video put together.

Well, actually, the trickiest part was watching Jonas, over and over again. I giggled when I saw the footage from the beach bonfire, Jonas looking at the camera over his shoulder every few minutes. I'd taken some clips of him while we were sailing, and now that I knew how his lips felt, I couldn't take my eyes off them. I'd filmed him sitting in the cockpit, gazing out over the ocean, and when he'd turned and caught me filming, his cheeks had pinked.

And that look on the dronie . . . I watched it over and over again.

James staggered into the kitchen and, bleary-eyed, started the coffee maker. I ignored him, focusing on my laptop and the clips and the music, trimming here and there while also adjusting the colors until I got the footage right.

Finally I'd done enough, and I took my headphones off and sat back.

"What time did you get up this morning?" James asked, leaning against the counter.

I stretched back in my chair. "Early, especially for Tahiti time." I checked my phone. "I can't believe we haven't heard from Mom yet."

He sipped his coffee and stared over the rim of the mug at me. "So, who were you talking to last night?"

Instantly I flushed. "None of your business."

"Mia," he teased me. "Did you find a hunky Polynesian man?"

"No."

"Polynesian woman?"

I rolled my eyes. "No."

He rolled his eyes right back. "Obviously it's another sailor." He set his mug down. "Tell me about him."

"There's nothing to tell." I got up and started shuffling around to make breakfast for the two of us, sliding some of James's god-awful bread into the toaster.

James helped me with breakfast. He diced fruit next to me in silence, a silence that hung over me.

"Jonas is nice," I finally said.

James put his knife down, crossed his arms, and looked at me. He studied me for a moment. I tried to ignore him, but a watched bread never toasts. "What?" I asked.

"Liam was nice."

I threw my hands up. "Holy shiitake, James, seriously? I'm not marrying him!"

"So what, then? You're scratching an itch?"

"Would that be so bad?" I challenged. "Are we gonna get a little hypocritical here? 'Cause I know you're no virgin."

"You know what it looks like to me?" James took a step closer.

I narrowed my eyes at him. "Watch yourself, James."

"It looks to me like you're scared. You're scared to go do this big adventure by yourself. You've complained to me about how shitty sailing is for women and now you're going to keep some guy around?"

"I'm not 'keeping him around.'"

"Oh, so what happens when you move west and you bump into him again? You've told me it's a small community."

I pressed my fingertips into my forehead. "James, what are you really getting at?"

"I'm just saying, you have to be careful. You're all alone on your boat and so far away from us. I don't worry about your sailing skills. I worry about those other people out there. What if someone hurts you again?"

And just like that, the anger whooshed out of me. "Aw, look at you, you big softy."

James grunted and turned away from me. I slid my arms under his and squeezed him from behind. "Is my widdle brother feeling protective?"

I felt him sigh. "It's not a joke, Mia."

"I know it's not." I pulled back and tugged on his shoulder until he turned around to face me. "I'm not getting into anything big, I promise."

Finally his shoulders collapsed and my brother wrapped me in a hug.

————

LATER, I WAS JUST BARELY FOLLOWING A CONVERSATION between Doug and Ike about property taxes in Seattle when my phone rang—Jonas was calling for a video chat. This was perplexing; we usually texted at night instead of during the day. I excused myself and climbed the stairs to find an empty bedroom, then answered the call.

"Hey, Jonas, is everything okay?"

Jonas came into focus and smiled. "Ja, everything is fine. But Marcella wanted to say goodbye." The camera panned over and I could see Marcella sitting next to Jonas.

"Hi, Mia!" she called out, and waved.

"Hey, girl! What's new? How did the interview go?"

"That's why we're calling. I got the job! They want me ASAP in Tivat, so I am flying out early tomorrow morning."

"Hey, congratulations!" I said. "That's so exciting." Marcella raved over the details, excited to get back to the Mediterranean and fine dining.

"I won't be here when you get back, but I wanted to say goodbye."

She blew me a kiss through the phone and I waved at her. Jonas came back into the shot and gave me a soft smile.

"Talk soon."

I hung up and stared at my phone. Marcella was leaving. Was *Eik* next?

TWENTY-FOUR

THE NEXT FEW DAYS WERE SPENT WITH THE FAMILY, AND most nights ended much later than I would normally stay up. The kids were often tucked into bed with a team effort by the adults—although my niblings had a particular interest in Uncle James tucking them in. When the basement was quiet enough, my mom would open a bottle or two of wine. By the time we made it back to James's place—once with the help of an Uber—it was late for us, but also late for Jonas. We hadn't talked for a few nights, but we had messaged occasionally.

James's words echoed through my mind when I considered calling Jonas. It was easier to be distracted.

Then a message came in while I was at my parents' house.

Can you talk now?

Instead of responding with a text, I placed a call and climbed the stairs to find an empty bedroom.

"Mia." Jonas's voice came through the phone, and I felt warm and fuzzy in my chest, even though I was pretty sure Jonas was calling to say they were moving on.

"Hi, Jonas."

"How is your family?"

I leaned back on one of the guest beds while I talked to Jonas, and he listened patiently. When I tired of family chat, I changed the subject. "Was there a particular reason you wanted to talk on the phone?"

"Yes, I have to talk to you about your boat." He cleared his throat. "*Eik* is going to move to Moorea tomorrow."

I sat up and swallowed hard. Moorea was a short sail away from Tahiti, but that would mean that Jonas would be gone. He wouldn't be there for me to see him when I got back, and they would probably move further west after that and I might never see him again.

"Oh" was all I could say.

"I was wondering, what if I stayed on your boat?"

"You would want to do that? But *Eik* would be moving without you."

"Yes, but Moorea is a short ferry ride away. So even if you do not sail over to Moorea, I can always get over there quickly."

"Why is *Eik* moving over there?"

"The crew is a little restless. Tahiti is not . . . There is not much here for us to do without a car. The other islands are more interesting, unless you are staying in a resort."

"Hmm. Well, if that's what you want to do, then yes, you should stay on *Welina*." I smiled broadly. "That would mean you would be waiting for me when I get back, hopefully."

"Ja. I would like that very much."

"Me too."

We said our goodbyes. Jonas went back to his crew and I rejoined my family.

———

JAMES HAD A WORK DINNER, AND INSTEAD OF SPENDING time with my family—I loved them very much, but after almost a week I was exhausted—I opted to stay at James's house and watch Netflix, another Stateside treat.

In the middle of a fluffy rom-com movie, I'd texted Jonas.

Are you around?

He hadn't answered, so James came home to find me on the couch working through a second movie—one that had me pulling in a box of tissues.

"What are you watching?"

I sniffed and blew my nose, pausing the movie so the title popped up.

James rolled his eyes. "No thank you. I'm going to bed."

He climbed the stairs, leaving me with my sob-fest on the couch, but a few minutes later my phone pinged.

Just got back from dinner. Are you still up? Jonas texted.

Yes, want to talk?

I hurried to turn off the TV and make it to my room. I flopped down on the bed just as the phone rang, but not a voice call, a video call. I looked around quickly and sat on my bed, fluffing some pillows and straightening my tank top. I clicked accept, and there was Jonas, settling into my bed, on my pillow, with the trappings of my home behind him.

He smiled at me.

"Where did you go to dinner?"

Jonas told me about friends he had made in the marina, more sailors passing through, a family on a catamaran, and sundowners that had turned into potluck.

I smiled while he yawned and stretched, the sheet slipping down his chest and pooling at his waist. "I like seeing you in my bed."

Jonas turned his head and smirked at me. "I like being in your bed. It smells like you and is soft and warm."

"Memory foam."

"It is better than memory foam. It is you."

My eyes slipped down his torso while he set up a pillow for his head and lay sideways. The sheet dipped dangerously low, showing an edge of hip and lean abs. "Are you naked in my bed?"

Jonas lifted his head and looked at me, surprised. "No." He was quiet for a moment. "Would you like me to be?"

I leaned back against the headboard and propped the phone on my knees. In the picture-in-picture, I could see my bottom lip disappearing between my teeth. "Yes."

Jonas sat up quickly, his phone falling flat against the bed, and I could barely see a hand, an elbow, the sheets, a wild scramble until Jonas returned, wide-awake and smiling. "Now I am naked for you."

Jonas was still holding the camera at such an

angle that I could only see the top of his chest. He quirked an eyebrow at me. "You too?"

I grinned and put my phone down, stripping out of my clothes and sliding under the covers. When I picked up the phone again, I was on my side, the sheet tucked in under my arms and covering my naked body.

Jonas tsk-tsked when he saw me. "Sexy and beautiful but not naked."

"Speak for yourself."

With one hand, Jonas reached past the camera, and though I couldn't see anything beyond his forearm, his body tensed and a quick inhale of air passed his lips.

Jonas's muscles slowly flexed and released, a slow, confident stroke. He bit his lip, staring just off-center at me, gauging my reaction.

I raised my hand close to my head, wiggled my fingertips, and tucked my hand under the sheet. Spreading my legs, I dipped my fingers in briefly and let my eyes roll back a little bit.

Jonas groaned.

Why were we teasing each other like this? I never thought of myself as a particularly shy or body-conscious person, but here I was, withholding a piece of myself. But so was he. Jonas had a fantastic body, and I wanted to see it so badly, but this way, I could focus on his eyes, his lips, his reactions to his hand and my own.

"Mia," he growled. "Oh, Mia."

I watched enraptured as Jonas's arm moved, his bicep flexing while his hand stroked. His breath was all I could hear, catching and rasping.

My fingers dipped and swirled, spreading my wetness around. My eyelids wanted to close, my body to sink into the pleasure, but I waited.

Jonas stroked faster, and I increased my pace too. That tightness started to build inside me, like a cramp I needed to shake off before my body snapped. We were both panting hard now, little moans and gasps being exchanged.

Suddenly, with my fidgeting and squirming, the sheet slipped off my breast and Jonas could see my nipple, tight and firm. "Oh fuck, Mia." He threw his head back, grunted, and then his body twitched, abs flexing and arms shaking as he came.

I was still crawling closer and closer to the edge. I could no longer manage to keep the phone angled correctly, but Jonas didn't complain.

"Almost there," I panted.

"God, Mia, you are so sexy like that. I want to hear you. Come for me."

Those words, and the longing in his voice, pushed me over the edge and I came hard against my hand.

For a few minutes I kept my eyes closed and listened to our breathing even out. When I could manage to move, I turned to my side and fished my phone out of the mess of sheets.

Jonas looked back at me from the screen. He gave me a soft smile. "You should go to bed now."

"Yeah," I agreed. "I would rather talk to you, though."

He chuckled. "Don't worry, we will talk tomorrow. Ja?"

"Ja," I said back to him. He smiled at my use of his native tongue.

"Good night, Mia."

"Night, Jonas."

———

I WAS BRAIDING LILY'S HAIR WHEN MOM CLAPPED HER hands.

"Clan, let's get together around the TV!"

I glanced over at Miranda, who was braiding Erica's hair. "What's going on?"

She gave me a look. "We all got the alert about your new episode, Mia. Guess what we're doing today?"

"What, really? Mom, it's not even a real episode."

"I don't care. You posted a video and the family's all here, so we're going to watch it."

I leaned over to Miranda. "It's, like, seven minutes long."

"It's okay, we're used to it." She patted Erica on the shoulder and stood up.

"Does she do this every time?"

"Come on, you know Mom attends *anything* her kids or grandkids do. Remember when she flew to attend Tyrell's kindergarten graduation and we all had to sit down and tell her she could not fly around for every little thing?"

The family members who were in the living room took up every available seat. Kids were nudging one another and wrestling around on the floor, Miranda sat in Doug's lap, and my brothers congregated near the kitchen.

"Okay, everyone, hush. Let's watch Mia's episode."

Mom hit play and I watched the video roll. The stunning views of my boat in Kauehi made me homesick to be out wandering again. I pictured her lonely in her slip, but then shook myself. She had Jonas to look after her.

The last shot was the dronie of Jonas and me waving and the drone zooming out. I kept the speed in real time for about four seconds before it soared out and faded to black.

"Jesus, Mia, that was beautiful. No wonder you wanted to go back to the boat."

"That looked like a dream vacation."

"Who was the guy at the end?"

James turned to me. "Yeah, Mia, who *was* the guy at the end?" When I stuck my tongue out at James, he laughed and turned back to the TV, picking up the remote.

"Jonas is a *friend*."

James coughed out, "Phone sex," and I felt my face heat up. I kicked his shin.

"No violence in front of the kids," Miranda called out, which of course made the kids all turn to look at me.

I sat on the arm of the couch next to James and pressed my shoulder to his. "Violence is bad, kids. And don't do drugs." I reached under James's arm and pinched his ribs.

James yelped and swatted my hand away. But it was Ike who interrupted us.

"Whoa, whoa, whoa. Mia, when did you upload this video?"

"Yesterday, why?"

He pointed at the screen. "It's got over a hundred

thousand views. And hundreds of comments. Holy shit."

"Ike!"

"Shiitake! Holy shiitake!"

James gave me a lopsided grin. "I guess Ike hasn't been keeping up with your videos, Mia."

"Yeah, Uncle Ike," Tyrell chimed in. "Aunt Mia is kind of a big deal."

Ringing endorsement from a teenager.

"Wait a minute." James narrowed his eyes. I looked at the screen and saw him scrolling through the comments section.

"James, don't go there."

"What the hell are these"—I elbowed him— "fudgepuckers thinking, saying sh . . . shih tzus like this!"

"That's why you don't read the comments section. At a certain point it gets too bad."

"I mean, at least they're not saying mean things about Mia?" Erica said.

"No, they're just a bunch of regular internet morons." James gritted his teeth.

"Okay, that's enough. Who wants to go for a ride in Uncle James's sports car?"

I left the room laughing, with a bunch of kids clamoring to get James to pick them first.

TWENTY-FIVE

Two days later I was at my parents' house. The day prior had been Crackers's service. Crackers's kids—all seven of them—had each gotten a chance to speak. Her friends from church and bingo had kept all the family busy, shaking hands with the adults and pinching the cheeks of the kids. My cousin Leo had booked a private room at an Irish pub afterward, and all of us grandkids had gone out and swapped stories. While the ones with kids had trickled out as the evening progressed, the rest of us with no obligations at home stayed out far too late.

Thus I was now nursing a hangover in my mother's kitchen.

James, also hungover, and I had barely made it over in time for the end of Family Breakfast, the last meal we all had together to say goodbye before everyone left. Dawn's family was first to go, as they had a flight to catch back east. Tyrell, who'd barely strung together six words the entire time I was there, asked if he could come visit me for spring break. Dawn's eyes had widened behind him.

"It's a lot like camping," I'd said.

He'd looked at me thoughtfully. "But there are beaches, right?"

"Yeah." Dawn had glared at me over his shoulder. "I'm not really sure where I'll be this spring, but why don't you discuss it with your parents and email me?"

That had placated both of them, and with hugs and kisses dispensed, they all took off for the airport. Hunter and his kids drove south a few minutes later, and with their cousins gone, the Seattle faction of my niblings dejectedly trudged back to their respective houses.

Mom sat James and me down with mugs of strong coffee at the kitchen bar and went about setting her kitchen to rights. She grabbed a plate with a few pieces of bacon left on it and handed it to us. "Finish this."

That was also how James and I dispatched the last biscuit and pieces of fruit. The coffee and food did the trick, and I was feeling much less queasy. We joined Mom and helped put the kitchen back in order.

No sooner were we done than Mom started pulling out baking supplies.

"Mom, what are you doing?" James asked. "We just cleaned."

She shrugged at him. "Sean has a soccer game this week. I told Miranda I'd make cookies."

Exasperated, James stomped down the stairs to clean the basement.

Mom watched him disappear and hummed. "Jonas is handsome."

I choked on my coffee.

"He's the one in the video, right?"

"Yes, Mom, he is."

She handed me a bowl and a measuring cup before cracking an egg into the mixer. "Two cups of flour. You'll see him when you get back to the boat?"

"Yeah, he's staying on *Welina* right now."

She nodded. "Are you changing your plans because of him?"

"My plans?"

"You said you didn't know where you were going to be in the spring."

"Oh, right. Jonas's boat is moving west to get to New Zealand by cyclone season."

She cocked her head at me. "And you're still planning to stay behind in French Polynesia?"

"Yeah, it's a good place to hang around for a while, get used to being by myself. But spring break is right around the shoulder season. I should be ready to head west myself then, and I would need to be flexible with my schedule."

She sighed. "I don't want you to miss an opportunity to be with someone because you don't think you're ready. You've been a sailor all your life. You were born ready to sail in the islands."

"Mom, come on. Jonas is great, but . . ."

When I didn't finish my sentence, she paused and stared at me. "But?"

I blew out a sharp breath. "People have . . . people have expectations, right? Like Dad, who's so supportive of me sailing by myself. It's great that he doesn't want me to give up my dream, and I don't want to disappoint him. But, sailing solo *sucks*. Where's the fun of sharing an experience with someone you love? I don't want to give up on my dream, but it's so *lonely*. And it's not a good solution to sail off into the sunset with someone because you like them. I mean"—I raised my arms out in a what-the-fuck gesture—"I know what it's like to sail with someone you know and love and look how that turned out."

By the time I'd finished my rant, I was huffing and Mom was looking at me with sympathy.

"Oh, honey."

"Not that"—I closed my eyes—"not that Jonas is even asking or it's even something I want to do. But spending time with anyone at this point is not dating."

My mom put the bowl down and reached out for me. I sidled in and wrapped my arms around her waist.

"It sounds like you are confused right now, Mia. And I hate to think of you stressing over all these things half a world away." She petted my hair. "But I can at least offer you this. Your dad, while he loves the idea of you sailing by yourself, he's scared too. He's scared that even doing his best, he couldn't protect you. So"—she pulled away—"your father is proud of you, as am I. And when life throws you lemons in the form of a good-looking man, make lemonade. Even if it's only temporary."

I blinked and pulled back. "Mom, is that a really bad metaphor for friends with benefits?"

"I believe it was a metaphor for orgasms, dear. Now help me finish getting these cookies in the oven."

———

MY KNEE BOUNCED, PROBABLY ANNOYING THE passenger beside me, but I didn't care. I was so anxious to get off this plane and see Jonas. The time apart had been harder than I'd expected. Jonas and I had only grown closer while I was gone, with hot phone conversations and sweet text message chats. I was so keen to get my hands on him.

The plane unloaded and I walked on the hot and sticky tarmac to the terminal. Tahiti's airport was small, so it was easy to find the baggage claim and get all the luggage shuffled out.

When I had my things, I smoothed my dress—I might have dressed up a little for Jonas in a sleeveless jersey sundress—and walked out into the lobby. There was that weird apprehension in the pit of my stomach trying to figure out how this would go. We'd kissed once, but over the past two weeks we'd talked every day, seen each other naked, watched each other come.

Would we hug, peck, swoon?

Immediately I spotted Jonas, his hair loose and shaggy around his face, a huge smile waiting for me. All the worries melted away as he stretched his arms out and enveloped me in a giant hug. I loved the way his body curved over mine, pulling me in close.

When he pulled back, Jonas's smile softened and he touched my hair. It was down and loose too. He stroked it once, his smile becoming something hot and laced with meaning. He pulled me in and took my mouth.

I didn't know how long we stood there giving each other soft, tender kisses, but finally we broke apart.

"How was your flight?" Jonas hefted one of my bags over his shoulder. He looked down and then grabbed the new, third bag. "Boat parts?"

"Yeah."

He nodded and slung it over his shoulder.

"The flight was good. Two movies and a window seat. It was nice to fly over Tahiti in the daylight again."

We worked our way to the taxi stand and climbed into a waiting car, giving the marina as our destination. Jonas pulled me in close to him and we leaned against each other.

I yawned and asked him about *Eik* and how his crew was doing.

"With Marcella gone, I think it's a little quiet. They will meet us at Moorea tomorrow, if that works for you?"

I nodded and looked up at Jonas. "How are you taking it?"

"It is okay. I have been lonely. I am glad you are back."

We unloaded at the dock and climbed onto *Welina*. I sighed, seeing the tired wood paneling and the various dings and dents around my boat.

Jonas and I chatted while I unpacked my clothes. I kept pulling out random food items, stuff I wasn't sure I could get in Tahiti but was a special treat from home.

I held up a box of Snoqualmie Falls Lodge pancake mix. "Have you had proper American pancakes before?"

"No. Have you had lutefisk before?"

I scrunched up my nose. "If you can find lutefisk, I'll eat it. But we have proper American pancakes, so you'll just have to suffer through these first."

The items on the galley counter piled up, but so did a stack of boat supplies. Jonas looked over everything.

He held up an item. "What is this for?"

I looked at him, perplexed. "It's the hose to fix that leak."

"Ah, you do not have to fix that."

"What do you mean?"

"I took care of it while you were gone."

I put my hands on my hips. "I know how to replace a thru-hull hose."

"Yes, of course. But I was here and I had time." He spread his hands out. "Was this okay?"

"Yes, I . . . Yes. I really appreciate that, Jonas."

I bent and kissed him. When I straightened up, he wrapped his arms around me, looking up and resting his chin on my stomach.

"I missed you."

"I missed you too. Thank you for leaving your crew and staying behind to be here."

He touched the tip of his finger to my nose, and I smiled at the gesture of affection I was becoming so used to. "Finish your unpacking."

I put things away, spare parts wedging into cabinets and tools finding their new homes.

When everything was where it belonged, I slumped onto the couch next to Jonas. "Okay, all done!" I turned to look at him, and he smiled at me. "We need to leave pretty early tomorrow morning to make it to Moorea by nightfall. That probably means an early morning tomorrow to get going." I yawned again. "Unfortunately, I need to go to the Carrefour and get some food."

"To Carrefour, then!"

We went to the supermarket and I was overwhelmed by the choices. This was the best selection I'd had to stock up the boat since Mexico, years ago. Jonas was helpful, pushing a second cart behind me as I loaded up piles of food.

Thankfully, the Carrefour allowed sailors to bring

the carts to the marina, a ten-minute walk away, where there was a designated drop-off area. However, the sidewalk was uneven and narrow, and even with the fading day, I was breaking a sweat and the jet lag was starting to catch up to me.

By the time we put my groceries away, my head was heavy, fatigue hitting me hard. Jonas cooed over me, force-fed me a sandwich, and sent me off to bed. I slept hard, not even waking when Jonas crawled into bed with me.

TWENTY-SIX

In the morning, I rolled over toward Jonas, who was asleep next to me. He was bathed in the morning light, hair loose and soft over the pillow.

I reached out and carefully touched his hair. Without opening his eyes, Jonas pulled me into his warmth. We lay like that for a while, Jonas stroking my back, my fingers tangled in his hair.

His breathing was still deep and even; I might have thought he was still asleep. But his fingers kept a lazy rhythm, and with our bodies pressed together, I could feel him growing hard.

I thought back to our video chats and the way Jonas looked when he came. I wanted to see it again, but this time to experience the heat and electricity in person. The more I thought about it, the more I could feel my body warming up. I fidgeted a bit against him, brushing against his hard cock more than once.

He groaned and tapped a finger against my spine. "Mia, the day must start."

"Does it have to? I'm so comfy right now." I kissed his bare chest and wriggled—brushing my thigh against him again—up his body to kiss his collarbone, his neck.

A groan vibrated over my lips. Jonas reached down, hooking the outside of my leg and wrapping it over his hip, which pushed me up the mattress a little bit. Reaching behind me, he skimmed the inside of my thigh with his palm, brushing the center of my panties with his fingertips.

He tilted his chin up and met my lips for a soft, tender kiss. His fingers stroked again, ever so gently, and I whined in impatience. I felt his lips tilt up, and he pressed a kiss more firmly.

I wiggled my hand between us, cupping his cock in my palm, and began to stroke him through his briefs. Jonas grunted and pressed his fingers harder into me. The cotton texture kept friction against me, and it didn't take long for us to both be panting and thrusting against each other's hands.

When I pulled my hand back, Jonas's body arched, chasing me. I chuckled and fumbled with the waistband of his briefs. The back of my fingers brushed over his ab muscles before I gripped him firmly.

Jonas's fingers froze and he sucked in a breath of air. I gave him a few strokes and he shuddered.

His torso twisted over mine, his mouth on me and his fingers pressing with more leverage from behind. Twisting, he pulled my panties to the side and plunged in.

I hiked my leg further up his waist and pressed us closer, trapping my hand and his cock between our bodies. I still gripped him, gently rocking my hand.

Jonas drove himself harder, his hips starting to thrust into my hand, his fingers pressing deeper into me.

With a cry, Jonas came in my hand, his hips thrusting and his head thrown back, fingers stilling inside me. I pumped him through his orgasm, and he collapsed underneath me.

We lay quiet, his warm breath washing over me. His cum was on my top and his stomach, making a sticky mess out of us. Jonas was recovering when suddenly I couldn't help it; I clenched on his fingers.

"Oh fuck." Jonas withdrew quickly, rising onto his knees and grabbing at the sides of my underwear. He yanked them down and thrust his fingers back in.

He pumped his fingers and I rode his hand until I came hard, crying out and bucking.

Jonas flopped over onto his back next to me. We both caught our breath, bodies limp and satiated.

———

I KNEW JONAS WAS ANXIOUS TO GET BACK TO HIS CREW and his own boat. I checked out with the marina and Jonas helped me get the boat off the dock. It was a gloriously beautiful day, the sun shining and a light breeze pushing us toward Moorea. Together, we raised the sails, *Welina* slipping gracefully through the water.

I looked at my charts to set the proper course. I could see that the island was surrounded by reef, but there was not much space between the reefs and the island.

"Which anchorage is *Eik* in?"

Jonas moved the screen around and showed me a deep bay with an open entrance through the reef. "Cook's Bay."

I set my autopilot to head to the entrance, then sat back in my seat.

"What have your crew been doing on Moorea?"

"They have been hiking and snorkeling. There is a small resort and a street to the east of the bay, full of beach bars and *pensions*. They have been waiting for us to go find the stingray feeding station."

"What's that?"

"The resorts have a spot where they go with their guests and feed the stingrays while swimming. It is quite the attraction."

I hummed. "That sounds great. I bet the snorkeling won't be anything compared to Fakarava, though."

Jonas twirled a finger in my hair and smiled. "Probably not."

We talked in the cockpit while the boat sailed on. Moorea grew on the horizon, a steep island with rugged mountains.

The bay came into view and it was stunning. It was long and narrow and extended into the mountains, which climbed up either side. Deeper inland the center of the island towered over us, with a dusting of clouds at the top.

I made the turn into Cook's Bay and Jonas and I dropped the anchor. It only took a few minutes for *Eik* to spot us, and the crew immediately climbed into their dinghy. Jonas and I watched them approach from the deck of *Welina*. I turned to him.

"How are we going to play this?"

He looked at me, confused. "Play this?"

"Yeah. This is the first time we're seeing your crew as a . . ." The word *couple* died on my lips. Was I actually trying to have "the talk"?

Jonas raised an eyebrow. A smile crept onto his lips. "As . . . ?"

I rolled my eyes, blushing furiously and trying not to smile. The dinghy was getting closer and Lila waved at me.

Jonas came to my side and pressed against me. "Mia," he said softly.

I looked at him out of the corner of my eye, suddenly shy that everyone was to know about us. He slid a hand across my cheek, turning my face toward him. He pressed a soft kiss to my lips. "They will know one way or another." He bent his head again, this time encouraging me to open for a deep, possessive kiss.

I felt the dinghy bump into *Welina*.

We broke apart to whistles and catcalls. Jonas reached down to help his brother tie up to *Welina*, and I welcomed everyone on board. Lila threw her arms around me in a tight hug. Eivind kissed both of my cheeks. And Elayna fumbled for a moment, her smile not quite reaching her eyes, but she recovered enough to give me a brief hug.

They crowded into my cockpit and I gestured for them to sit. Jonas pulled me down to sit next to him, my bent leg overlapping his thigh, and his palm resting on the inside of my leg.

"How was your trip home?" Lila asked me.

"It was really good to see my family, of course. Everyone came in: my aunts and uncles, most of my cousins who live on the West Coast." We talked for a while about my family and my flights, and what they had been up to in the meantime.

Eivind leaned back, resting his arm behind Lila. "You are just in time. Tomorrow night they have a dance show at the hotel on the water." He pointed at the resort further into the bay. "They only do it once a week, so we should go."

"Yes!" Elayna exclaimed. "I hear the dancing show is not to be missed."

"A special treat, then." Jonas smiled.

"Okay." Elayna patted her thighs. "We made you a special welcome home dinner, Jonas. Let's get back to *Eik*."

Jonas and I looked at each other. We hadn't talked about tonight, but with a sinking feeling, I realized he needed to go back to his boat. The same thought was on his face: disappointment. He should catch up with his crew right now.

I followed Jonas back into my cabin while he packed. The ache in my chest was stupid; we'd shared a bed one night since I came back from the States. Jonas had his own boat and I had mine.

Jonas slung his bag over his shoulder and crowded me against the wall. I tilted my chin up as he pressed against me, my eyes focused on his lips. "I do not want to sleep without you tonight."

I huffed a laugh. "Addicted already?"

"Ja." His lips lightly brushed mine.

I took a deep breath and gently pushed him away. "Come on. I'll be here tomorrow and your crew is excited to have you back."

———

THAT NIGHT I HAD A QUIET DINNER IN MY COCKPIT. Despite having resupplied the boat, cooking a full dinner by myself in the quiet of *Welina* actually seemed pathetic. Maybe it was the contrast of my loud, rambunctious family, or maybe it was being torn from Jonas so quickly. I moped over a plate of cheese and crackers instead. The sounds of ruckus and laughter form *Eik* drifted over to me while I sat alone, bobbing in the Pacific Ocean.

TWENTY-SEVEN

"YOU AND JONAS SEEM COZY NOW." LILA NUDGED ME with her hip. We were taking a first pass through the buffet line and filling our plates with some local delicacies, some I'd heard of before and some I hadn't.

I blushed. "Yeah, I guess we are."

"Did absence make the heart grow fonder?"

"Something like that."

We wove our way through the tables lit with tiki torches in the open air. There was a small band playing, a mix of men and women, Tahitians wearing traditional costume and dress. The women wore intricate woven headdresses made of dried fibers and flowers, bandeau tops, and lush vibrant skirts made of leaves. The men were shirtless, built, and heavily tattooed, wearing pareos and braided bands on their biceps and calves.

While we ate, we caught up on the activities Eivind and the rest of the crew had done on the island.

"You can hike through the pineapple plantations to a viewpoint overlooking the bay. It is pretty high up," Eivind said.

"We also went to the juice factory," Lila chimed in. "They make a juice mix in a carton, perhaps you saw it at the store? It has alcohol in it already, and vanilla. It is too sweet, a hangover waiting to happen."

"Where is Elayna?" Eivind asked. She hadn't returned from the buffet yet.

Lila swallowed her bite of food. "Is that her by the bar?"

We all looked to see Elayna chatting with a tourist at the bar. She was already at the bottom of her drink, and as we watched, the bartender replaced it with another.

Jonas and Eivind exchanged glances. "She needs to eat," Jonas said. He started to get up from the table, but Lila stopped him.

"I think I should go talk to her."

A few minutes later Lila returned without Elayna. She shrugged. "She says she is fine."

Jonas's brow furrowed and I felt the tiniest bit of jealousy at his concern over Elayna—but I reminded myself Jonas was in my bed at night. They'd been separated for over a week now, and it was normal for Jonas to be concerned for his friend, especially a crew member on his boat.

Shortly after we'd finished eating, the dancers started up. First there was a fire dance show with three oiled Tahitian men in traditional woven skirts and armbands.

They climbed and jumped over one another, shouting and twirling their double-ended fire batons at the same time. It was mesmerizing and when I blinked, the circles of fire danced in my vision.

I leaned into Jonas, who put his arm around me. "Impressive, no?"

I nodded. "Not something I want to try to pick up on the boat."

Next were a troupe of women in long loose skirts and headdresses embellished with flowers. Their movements were graceful and flowing, accompanying the wistful song playing from the band.

The last dance of the night was couples. The beat picked up and the women gyrated their hips to the music, making the edges of their skirts flip up and sway. The men made all kinds of noises and leaped about.

Finally, with a loud chant from everyone, the

music ended and the dancers struck their poses, their skin slicked with sweat and flickering in the firelight.

We clapped for the dancers and they gestured for guests to come up and open the dance floor. There were dance lessons and posed photos, and in the crush of people, Jonas and I lost track of the rest of the crew.

He slipped his hand into mine and pressed me back against him. His breath was warm in my ear. "Want to go home? I will ask Eivind to drive us back?"

I nodded, excitement fluttering in my belly. In the darkness and flames, Jonas glowed.

We threaded through the crowd until we found Eivind, who nodded and took us home in the dinghy.

We climbed aboard *Eik*, waved goodbye to Eivind, and I stepped into Jonas's cabin for the first time. It was remarkably tidy and neat, everything stashed in cabinets and shelves, unlike my messy cabin.

"Wow, do you even live here? Where's all your stuff?" I teased.

Jonas came up behind me and wrapped his arms around my waist. "I have plenty of things. My boat is just a little bit tidier than yours," he teased.

I shivered when he brought his mouth to my ear and tugged on my earlobe. The press of his body behind me was warm and comforting. He slid his hands down my sides, the tips of his fingers barely touching the skin at the edge of my dress.

When I stretched my arms over my head and placed my hands on Jonas's neck, the bottom of my dress slid higher, and Jonas took the invitation to skim his hands up my thighs. He hiked my skirt up further, trailing light fingers over the tops of my thighs until he reached my panties.

My heartbeat picked up, racing in my chest. I let my fingers spread and play with Jonas's hair while he skimmed his fingers back down again, as far as he could reach.

Jonas's lips touched my neck and he left wet kisses trailing down my flesh. My breath hitched when his fingers came back up. They slipped carefully under the band of my underwear at my hips. He stroked, ever so carefully, over my delicate skin.

His arms were pressing me back into his body, and I could feel the firmness of his erection against my butt.

When his fingers started to circle closer to my center, I had to grip his forearm to try to control myself. Jonas froze.

"Do you want me to stop?"

"God, no."

He pressed his chuckle into the soft spot behind my ear.

Jonas shifted around me, his left arm snaking up the rest of my dress to flatten his palm over the center of my chest. His right hand slipped closer toward me, his fingers divided, and he kneaded the flesh on either side of my slit.

He wasn't directly touching my clit; instead he lightly played with me there, amping me up. I bucked and he squeezed his arm tighter, pulling me back into his chest.

"You don't have to be quiet," he whispered. "We have the boat all to ourselves."

I moaned and he grunted back at me. He moved his left hand over to my nipple and gave me a little pinch that had me bucking again and moaning louder. Gently, he guided me back until he leaned on the door and I was pressed against him.

His fingers slipped lower and he was finally touching my clit. He stroked with two fingers, trapping me between them and applying pressure.

"What do you need?"

I gasped and felt an ache starting up in my center. "Harder."

Jonas pressed more firmly, sliding and stroking and kneading my body until I was chasing the big finish.

Then suddenly the boat rocked hard beneath us. When we stilled, we could hear the drone of a dinghy engine nearby. We both froze, waiting to see if we were about to have company.

When we heard voices and felt the bump of the dinghy hitting *Eik*'s hull, we both collapsed together in disappointment. We listened for a few moments as voices got louder and we heard the heavy tread of steps on the deck.

Jonas kissed my hair. "We can be quiet."

"Yeah," I breathed out.

He started stroking again, the rest of his crew a thin door away. I bit my lip and focused on chasing that ache again.

But then something hit the door with a thunk, and Jonas froze.

On the other side of the door, the voices were rising. Lila cajoled, ". . . water, before you . . . need the head . . .bucket, Eivind."

Jonas was tense behind me, torn between me and his crew.

"I think you should go out there and take care of things. Your crew needs you."

Jonas slipped his hand out of my panties and pressed a quiet kiss to my shoulder. With both hands on my hips, he guided me toward the bed.

"Wait in my bed?" he whispered.

I nodded and slipped into the sheets. Jonas turned on a bedside light and then turned off the cabin lights before he opened the door and went into the salon.

Straining my ears, I could hear raised voices, the deep cadence of Jonas's and the higher, nearly shrill voices of the others. I couldn't make out the words, so I lay back on the pillow and tried to sleep.

———

SOMETIME LATER I WOKE UP TO JONAS SLIPPING UNDER the sheet with me and turning out the light. When I rolled toward him, he slipped his hand to my waist and stroked my hair in the darkness.

I opened my mouth and rasped in a sleep-worn voice, "Is everything okay?"

"It will be," he said. "Elayna is drunk and not herself. We will talk more in the morning. Go to sleep."

I turned away from Jonas and he wrapped his arm around me, tugging me in toward his body. I fell back to sleep.

TWENTY-EIGHT

IN THE MORNING, I BLINKED AWAKE AND SAW JONAS next to me, still asleep. The fan in his cabin rotated on the opposite wall, blowing over my skin every few seconds. Jonas was bathed in the sunlight streaming in from the window behind him. I watched him sleep for a little while, drowsing on and off myself. Then I felt him shift, his hand pressed into the small of my back, a huff of breath over my cheek.

"Good morning," I whispered. I got a muffled grunt in response. Jonas's fingers stretched over my back, tugging me closer. When I opened my eyes, his face was pushed into the crevice between our pillows.

I scooted closer and he wrapped an arm around my waist. I lightly ran my nails over his scalp, combing his hair and pushing it to the side so I could see his face. "You were up late last night. Is everything okay with Elayna?"

He sighed and pushed himself up. "Elayna got too drunk. The man she was spending time with told her to go home and she got upset. We had to calm her down; she was yelling and crying, making a scene."

"Does this happen often?"

He shook his head. "I have never seen her like that."

I sat up and stretched my arms over my head and then pressed my hand onto the bed next to Jonas, looking down at him. "Is this something to do with you and me?"

Jonas scratched his chest, his eyes on the ceiling as he considered my question. "No . . . I . . . maybe?" He shook his head, focusing his eyes on me. "I do not know where this is coming from. I think something is going on with her. Elayna drank a bit too much one night in Tahiti while you were gone, and Eivind mentioned something last night about an incident here before we arrived."

I dropped down to my elbow and trailed a finger on Jonas's chest. "I think you need to have some more crew time today."

He slid his palm over my hand. "Ja. But I missed you. I want you to be here too."

"I know. But this is your crew—and your brother. You need to take care of them. It's one of the things I like about you." I slipped my hand from his and traced a finger over his eyebrow. "You have such a good relationship with Eivind, and Lila and Elayna both admire you. And so do I. If Elayna's going through something, you can help her. She'd listen to you; she respects you."

"You have high expectations of me." A small crease of worry formed between his eyebrows and I kissed it away.

"I know you, Captain. Now"—I threw off the sheet and rolled out of the bed—"take me home and take care of your boat."

———

I stayed on *Welina* all day, letting Jonas and the rest of *Eik* have a day together to sort out their shit. Jonas and I had just spent several days together, but I still missed him, and I tried hard not to think too much about him. I had plenty of boat projects to keep me entertained, projects that I now had the right parts for.

Shortly after I ate lunch, *Eik*'s dinghy bumped into *Welina* and Jonas climbed aboard.

I met him at the base of the stairs. "Is everything okay? I didn't expect you to come over today."

He paused, reached back outside, and pulled in two coconuts. "These are for you."

I smiled and took the coconuts from him and shoved them into my fridge. Jonas sat on the stairs. "You know you don't have to butter me up anymore." I leaned in for a kiss. "I like you with or without the coconuts."

"Actually, Elayna insisted I bring these over to you. As an apology for last night."

"Aw, that was nice of her. Tell her thank you."

He took a deep breath. "Elayna is leaving *Eik*. We sat down and had a talk, and she apologized to the rest of us. She is embarrassed about last night and has decided it would be best for her to move on now."

I looked out the window and tried to sort out my feelings over his statement. Compared to the rest of the crew, I wasn't as close with Elayna, and she seemed to be really struggling with something, maybe my relationship with Jonas, given their history, or maybe her life in general. A pang of sympathy hit me. I knew how it felt to be a little lost and unsure and to have your heart and mind disagree. "How do you feel about that?"

He rubbed his face, and when he pulled his hands

away, his eyes were tired. "Sad. We have lost both of our crew members in a few weeks. And I feel at fault."

I stood between Jonas's knees and gripped his wrists, tugging his arms around me and letting him rest against me. "You gave both Marcella and Elayna great opportunities. Just think about where they were before they met you."

He huffed a laugh into my chest. "Elayna was desperate to get away from that drunkard, and Marcella had just been fired."

"Exactly. And now they've had a stable home for months and these amazing travel experiences. And Marcella has a fancy new job. Elayna will find something. She'll land on her feet, better off than she was before because of you."

Jonas squeezed me hard, burying his face into me. "Thank you," he said, his voice muffled. I held him until he pulled back. He glanced over my shoulder at the clock mounted on the wall. "I should go. We are taking Elayna to shore to meet the three p.m. ferry for Papeete."

I helped Jonas into his dinghy and watched him putter away. To my surprise, the dinghy returned later, laden with the crew of *Eik* and Elayna's bags. She picked her way over the bags and climbed aboard *Welina*, smiling at me shyly.

"I just wanted to say goodbye. It was lovely to meet you, and you never know when our paths will cross again." She held out her arms for a hug, and I wrapped mine around her.

"It was great to meet you too. Go have some great adventures, okay?"

I started to pull back, but Elayna gripped me tighter. I tensed, but she whispered in my ear, "Take good care of him, okay?" and then she kissed my cheek.

"I'll try."

She smiled, her eyes misty. "And take care of you." She gave me a little wave and climbed back down to the waiting crew. I waved them off as they puttered to the dock.

———

JONAS RETURNED IN THE LATE AFTERNOON AND SPENT the rest of the day being extra affectionate, needing every kiss or touch for reassurance. We cuddled and read in the hammock again, and Jonas suggested we do something fun the next day: snorkeling with stingrays and a double-date dinner on *Eik* with Lila and Eivind.

When I suggested he go home for dinner, he gave me a soft little smile and kissed my cheek.

"This is the first time in a while that Eivind and Lila have had the boat to themselves. I am not sure what I will be walking into," Jonas joked.

The next morning was quiet and I didn't see any sign of the crew on *Eik* while I drank my coffee and ate breakfast. I was excited to get out and do something fun. Jonas was right: this was what we needed.

I distracted myself by getting ready. There was no free diving today, we'd be in shallow waters for the stingray swim, so all I had to do was put a bathing suit on and sunscreen up. My snorkel and mask sat on the side deck, waiting.

The sound of a dinghy engine roaring to life hit me, and I watched as the crew of *Eik* filled the dinghy. They puttered over, and the dinghy seemed empty without their extra crew.

I passed my gear down and took a seat next to Jonas, wishing Lila and Eivind a good morning. Jonas kissed my cheek and squeezed my thigh before revving the dinghy up.

We had a long way to go. Conversation over the noise of the engine was impossible. Jonas steered us out of the bay and turned left, weaving our way between the reef and the island, following the band of sand below us. A few times we had to backtrack a little bit, careful not to run over coral where the water was too shallow, lest we damage the reef or the dinghy.

On the horizon we could see a few small boats anchored out at the reef. We motored up and, keeping some distance away from the swimmers, tossed our little anchor into the water.

Immediately we found ourselves being circled by thin dark shapes, two or three feet long.

"Eivind." Lila peered into the water nervously. "Those are not rays."

He bent over the side of the dinghy. "No, they are reef sharks. Just like we swam with in Fakarava."

"They are *really* close."

"See the black tip?" Jonas pointed. "They are black-tipped reef sharks. We see them all the time."

Lila did not look reassured. "It's very shallow here. In Fakarava it was deep and there were lots of fish and coral to look at." She chewed on her lip and eyed the water.

"You do not have to go." Eivind strapped his mask on, letting the snorkel dangle on the side of his head.

Jonas had his mask on too. He swung a leg over the side of the dinghy and slid into the water. I spun around and slipped in too, Jonas catching me in his arms, the slickness of the water making his hands glide against my skin.

It was shallow enough that I could stand and the water lapped at my shoulders. Jonas wrapped his arms around me, pressing my body against his.

Our masks knocked together and we laughed.

Until something slimy slithered up my leg.

I yelped and jumped up, wrapping my legs around Jonas. Lila screamed.

"It's okay!" I said, while Jonas laughed. "It was just a stingray."

I held on to Jonas with my legs, and we both put our snorkels in our mouths and put our faces in the water.

The stingray who'd touched my leg was gone, but more were on the way. Their large round bodies swooped above the sand as they circled us, exploring.

I heard the others jump into the water, and more stingrays started approaching. I watched as one flapped toward us, doing a drive-by and caressing Jonas's legs with his fin. Jonas laughed into his snorkel.

We continued to watch the rays as they grew bolder. One down on the sand nudged Jonas's foot, backed up, and nudged him again. When we didn't respond, the ray swam up Jonas's leg, flapping his wings and pressing his slick body against us.

With me in his arms, Jonas stepped back, letting the ray fall away from us.

We both raised our heads and spit our snorkels out, laughing. "Oh my God, that felt so weird!"

"They are slimy." Jonas wrinkled his nose in his mask.

We ducked back down and watched the rays more. They swam by, anywhere from the surface of the water to the sandy bottom, brushing us when they passed. It was hard to keep my hands to myself; I wanted to pet them. I detached from Jonas and stood on my own, but I had to fend off several rays that tried to climb up my body.

Once the rays calmed down a little bit, I looked around. There were still sharks nearby, but in the excitement of the rays I had completely forgotten about them. They circled the whole area, slowly keeping an eye on things.

They weren't the only ones: large, colorful coral fish circled as well, ducking in to pick at the sand occasionally.

The tour boats had a few people in the water, but most didn't want to get in and instead watched from above. Lila did eventually get in, but she clung to Eivind.

When the rays grew tired of us and my shoulders

were too warm from the sun, we climbed into the dinghy and puttered home.

————

Jonas picked me up an hour later. I was clean and dressed up in my jersey dress again for our double date. He whistled when he pulled alongside *Welina*.

On *Eik*, things had returned to normal again. Lila was in charge of the meal, but she quickly doled out tasks for everyone. We drank, we laughed, we were two couples enjoying one another's company.

And that night, Jonas and I slipped under the covers and used our hands to tease and torment each other.

————

After a lazy morning and breakfast, Lila and Eivind were eager to get off the boat for a hike. They invited Jonas and I to join them, but after exchanging raised eyebrows, Jonas diplomatically offered to drive them to shore.

"You didn't want to go?" I asked when he returned.

He raised an eyebrow. "Of course not. Not when I could have you all to myself."

We raced to Jonas's cabin. I turned around and found him already pulling me in, wrapping an arm firmly around my waist and taking my mouth in his. It was intense and frantic for a few minutes; we couldn't get enough of each other's mouths.

Jonas pulled away, taking some deep breaths. I kissed the hollow of his neck, and he slid an arm down to my bottom and picked me up. I wrapped my legs around his waist and held on to his shoulders. He found my mouth again, this time slower, taking his time with my lips. He kneeled on the bed and shifted our weight, gently putting me on my back.

We stretched out, our fingers tangling above my head. Jonas lined up perfectly with me, his hardness rubbing against me while we shifted.

So slow, achingly slow, Jonas showered me with kisses, licks, and nibbles. He rocked deep with his hips while maintaining eye contact, our open mouths brushing.

When he kissed me, I rocked up, pushing my hips back at him and rising off the bed. Jonas chuckled and let go of my hands. His lips pressed a trail down my chest until he got to my tank top.

His finger traced the edge and then slowly tugged the fabric down my arm until the hem caught on my nipple. He applied his mouth, stretching his tongue under the fabric and flattening it against me. I moaned and grabbed his head, holding him down.

Both straps came down, my top was around my waist, and Jonas was greedily sucking. He broke away and rasped, "You are so beautiful," before switching to my other breast.

I could no longer feel his cock between my legs; I had nothing to grind against anymore. Hearing my whimper of frustration, Jonas slid a hand down to cup me. He pressed, fumbling with the slick material of my athletic shorts until he had enough pressure to stay on just the right spot.

With a few circles, I was getting too close to the edge. "Jonas," I cried out. "Please!"

He crawled back up, covering my body with his, his warm chest pressing against my damp nipples as his teeth tugged on my ear. "Beautiful, come for me."

I tensed and his fingers kept their rhythm, and I went over the edge. My hips tilted with each pulse.

His fingers slowed and we caught our breath. Jonas was hard, pressed into my hip, but offering me sweet, tender kisses.

"I thought alone time meant we'd finally have sex."

He scoffed at me. "Ja, but not *only*."

We grinned at each other, and I tugged him down for another sweet kiss. I teased him, nipping and licking and backing away until he grunted and came down forcefully. He held my eyes for a moment, but I felt his hand snake over the waistband of my shorts, and suddenly he broke away, tugging them down my legs and taking my underwear with them.

When my bottoms were on the floor, I sat up and yanked my top over my head. Jonas stripped his clothes off in one swoop, climbing back over me to brace his arms on either side.

When he settled his weight against me again, I involuntarily hissed and bucked, my skin still sensitive. He backed off immediately. "Are you okay?"

"Yes, sorry, it was still sensitive for a moment. It's fine now."

He watched my face as he pressed back down, keeping his cock between our stomachs. When his weight was on me, we kissed more, grinding and straining against each other.

Finally I broke away. "Jonas, do you have condoms?"

His eyes rolled back. "Oh thank God." He pushed off me and fetched condoms from a cabinet across the room. I propped myself up to watch him slide the condom on.

He crawled over me and aligned himself. Jonas tangled his fingers in my hair, kissing me deeply before pressing gently into me.

We both lay there, relaxing into each other with him seated so deeply. Jonas took my mouth again and we began a rhythm: kiss, breathe, grind, gasp, arch, thrust. Over and over again, we made these deep, real imprints on each other.

Jonas panted harder, and his kisses became more sparse, his thrusts more uncontrolled. "Mia," he whispered. "Mia, Mia, Mia . . ."

Clenching, Jonas came, his gasps echoing in my ears.

TWENTY-NINE

WE LAY IN BED STROKING EACH OTHER, LIGHTLY touching, kissing and teasing while we relaxed on the bed. I traced the ridges of his chest as he stroked and twirled my hair around his fingers.

Suddenly there was a bump against the boat, followed by loud stomping across the deck.

"Jonas!" Eivind's voice shouted out.

Jonas's eyes widened. "Oh shit." He leaped out of bed, scrambling to throw clothes on. Confused, I followed suit and was halfway decent when the banging started on the door.

"What's going on?" I hissed at Jonas.

"I was supposed to have the radio on to pick them up from shore."

Eivind was calling through the door, sounding

pissed. When I was fully dressed, Jonas opened the door.

Eivind started talking rapidly in Norwegian and Jonas held his hands out, keeping a calm tone as he responded. Lila's eyes bounced back and forth between the two men until finally she smacked Eivind's arm with the back of her hand.

"Eivind, in English so I can yell too!"

That broke Eivind's anger, and his emotions drained away. He raked his hands through his cropped hair, then sat on the bench and put his face in his hands.

The whole boat was silent for a moment.

"I am sorry, Eivind." Jonas hung his head.

Eivind sighed and sat back, resting his arms on the table. "What are we doing?"

Jonas darted a glance at me. "We were, ah . . ."

Eivind let out a dark laugh. "No, Jonas, us." He gestured around the boat. "Elayna is gone, Marcella is gone, we have no new crew member. Lila's visa runs out in less than a week. There are still several islands between us and Bora Bora. We will have to skip them to get to Bora Bora to start the clearance formalities. And that is just the next week or so. The season will be over before we know it, and we will need to get to New Zealand in a rush."

"Ja. I know," Jonas said quietly. He hesitated and

looked at me. "If we leave tomorrow, to sail to Bora Bora, will you come?"

I knew what he was really asking me: How far would I go to stay with him? He would get his boat to New Zealand before cyclone season. If I moved far enough west past the invisible line, I was committing to going all the way to New Zealand. Every mile I went west would make it harder for me to sail back to safety.

And the only other option would be to sail *Welina* all the way to New Zealand. By myself.

"No."

The look on Jonas's face broke me. He was stunned.

"It is only a few days of sailing to get to Bora Bora."

"I know. I would be alone."

"You are a great sailor. You can solo sail—I know you can."

I looked at Jonas, his eyes pleading with me. "I know I'm a great sailor, Jonas. I know I can do it. But I don't *want* to. This is not just Bora Bora."

He stood in front of me, placing his hands on my shoulders. "You could come with us."

I shook my head. "You can't leave your boat, and I can't leave mine."

He swallowed thickly. Eivind quietly guided Lila back to their cabin, leaving us alone.

"So what do we do?"

I gripped his wrists. "We keep in touch, okay? We don't know what our plans are after this year—"

"My plans were to go back to Norway. I would rather be with you."

"We will keep in touch," I said, calmly but firmly. "You'll get your boat to New Zealand, and I'll sort out what I'm going to do with *Welina*. And we will talk more in November."

He closed his eyes and pressed his forehead against mine. His voice was almost a whisper. "I know that makes sense, but that is not what I want."

"I don't know of any other way to do it, Jonas," I pleaded with him. "My whole life is in my boat, all my money. I need time."

He nodded and sniffed, pulling back from me. "Maybe it is best that we leave in the morning for Bora Bora."

I nodded too. "Yeah. I think that would be good. You have to leave the country soon anyway. I will sail back to Tahiti tomorrow."

I stepped toward the companionway. "Can you drive me home?"

We climbed into the dinghy and Jonas fired it up.

He motored to *Welina*, and I tied his dinghy to my boat. "You have some things inside," I said.

He was behind me, following me, and a sense of urgency built until we were chasing each other into my cabin. Our mouths were on each other, nipping and biting while we tore our clothes off. I crawled backward, loath to stop kissing him. Jonas tried to come with me but smacked his head on the low ceiling above my bed.

It didn't faze him at all, and he dropped over me, wrapping his arms around me and pushing us back onto the bed.

He shifted to pull off his underwear, and I wriggled out of mine before freezing. "Jonas, I don't have any condoms."

"We do not do that, then." He returned to kiss me again. "I will do other things to you."

He rose up as high as he could and grabbed my foot, pulling my leg underneath him to spread me open. He buried his face between my legs and I gasped and arched my back.

Jonas was licking and sucking my flesh, winding me up and making me crazy. He pushed my knees up, spreading my legs further while he licked and teased. I shifted, grinding up, twisting my hips and chasing my orgasm when he backed off suddenly. I looked down to see him grinning up at me. He opened his mouth and gave me a lazy lick up my center, making my back arch off the bed.

"Jonas!" He chuckled and returned to give me a slow, open kiss. I didn't know how he was able to put the brakes on so hard when all I could think was *Go, go, go.*

He pulled back to watch me. Not my face, but my pussy. His hands had a firm grip on my waist, his shoulders holding me open.

"Jonas," I said, much more sternly. He flashed me a grin and licked again, a little faster this time. And again, pressing harder. A few swirls, flicks, and sucks and he backed off again and I groaned in frustration. I tried to reach down and tug at his hair but he evaded my hands.

He kept it up until I thought I was going to break. Even a little lick felt like it was going to send me over the edge. My body was so tense, so needy.

"Please," I whispered.

He slid his tongue over me, over and over and I was coming and coming so hard, I screwed my eyes shut and tried to remember to breathe because I had forgotten what my lungs were for.

Jonas eased his mouth around me carefully, gentle on my sensitive flesh. He slid up my body, and his cock and my hand found each other like magnets. I gave him soft strokes, teasing him in turn, but he got me back with these wide, deep kisses. I could taste myself on him and I wanted more.

I gripped him, holding him tight and stroking firmly. My body felt so quiet, so calm, it made me hear every sound he made: his heart beating faster, his breath hitching, his pulse under my palm fluttering.

Letting go of him, I pushed him onto his back and then bent down, letting the head of his cock slip into my mouth. I gave it a rough suck. His body bowed and he shouted something in Norwegian. I felt the tautness in him: Jonas was gritting his body and forcing himself not to come.

I pressed a kiss to the tip, and then a firm lick along his entire length. He begged me, giving up so quickly when he had held my pleasure for so long.

I wrapped my hand around him too and stroked him. "Harder, please, Mia . . ." he rasped.

So I did, I stroked him hard, and licked and sucked and took him over the edge mercifully quickly, swallowing him down.

He shuddered and groaned, making these wonderful little noises, noises I would never forget.

I crawled to him and he wrapped his arms around me.

———

WHEN I WOKE UP, JONAS WAS GONE. AND SOMETIME between cooking dinner and getting ready for bed, I looked up and *Eik* was gone. A flash of relief made its way through my body; I didn't think I had it in me to be the one to leave first.

THIRTY

For the next week, I tried to fit my life into some kind of normalcy again. What was normal? I flipped open books, but I'd find myself staring at the page, my eyes focused beyond the words. Boats came and went in the bay, and part of me secretly wished each sail on the horizon was *Eik* returning, but I knew time slipped on and Jonas was further away.

Liam had twined into my life slowly, and the extraction had been painful and drawn out. Jonas had come into my life with a splash, and out with a puff of breeze.

Unlike the rip of a Band-Aid, Jonas's disappearance got worse each day. I missed his calm presence, his small, tender smiles. Eventually, I knew, I would have to move *Welina* again, and having to do it without Jonas there to help me, to once again be alone, seemed like an insurmountable task.

My satellite device pinged. I rolled over on the settee, my eyes darting around the cabin. Where was my phone? I'd switched it off days ago to save money on the expensive cell phone service when I couldn't find a free Wi-Fi signal.

It was tucked under my logbook on the nav desk. I switched it on and connected directly to the sat.

Your dot hasn't moved, but you aren't answering my messages. Are you alive? Or is the kraken devouring ships in Moorea?

I rolled my eyes at James, and dutifully switched my phone onto the cell network. Pings filled the cabin as notifications popped up on my screen. I had twelve from James, including a photo of him holding up a bottle of kombucha and smirking.

I'm alive. No kraken here.

His message came back immediately. *Good. Will call off armada of kraken hunters. They never stood a chance anyway.*

Revenge killings of mythical beings rarely ever turn out well.

How's Jonas?

He left—I consulted the calendar—*last week. Bound for points west.*

Aw, Miamati, I'm sorry.

The screen showed my brother typing for a few moments, then the dots disappeared, then there was more typing, then not, then typing . . .

Hypothetically speaking, if one wanted to track down Jonas, where would one find him?

You can't fly halfway around the world to punch Jonas.

What's his boat name again?

You aren't tracking him on AIS either.

This was easier when you dated those schmucks in high school.

It was satisfying when you threatened Billy Radcliffe and he avoided me for the rest of senior year.

James didn't answer for a couple of minutes, so I flipped through my apps and caught up on messages. When I switched over to my personal email, I sat up straight. My inbox, normally pretty empty, had a slew of unread emails, a mix of messages from Jonas and *Eik*.

I opened the first one.

Mia, pulling up the anchor last night and sailing away from you was one of the hardest things I have ever done.

I greedily devoured every email he sent me. Some were sent from *Eik*'s at-sea email address, with updates on sailing (*We departed Bora Bora after only two days, taking advantage of the good weather, Eik is moving along at eight knots with the wind deep behind us, we expect to arrive tomorrow*), but they almost always included a peek into Jonas's mind.

We drank coconuts at Bloody Mary's, and I thought of you.

I came up for my night watch to find Lila and Eivind snuggling in the corner of the cockpit. I nearly turned Eik around to sail back to you.

Someday satellite technology will allow us to video chat across thousands of miles of ocean.

Each email was signed *Yours, Jonas.* I ignored my buzzing phone while I caught up, tears filling my eyes and blurring the screen. After reading the last email, dated mere hours ago, I pressed my face into a throw pillow and cried.

When I resurfaced, snotty and spent, I switched back to my chat with James. His messages waited not so patiently.

I would gladly fly across the ocean to threaten Jonas for you, but maybe I need to fly over and threaten you.

I just want you to be happy, Mia. I know Welina *means a lot to you, and you fought so hard for her, but I hate to think of you slipping back into a bad place.*

Mia?

Goddamn it. The kraken's back.

I'm sharpening my harpoon.

I snorted a little laugh, and typed a response.

I'm alive. Jesus. Step away from the harpoon. I've got

some emails I need to answer. Love you, hugs to the 'rents when you see them next.

An hour later I'd reread Jonas's emails, looked up his position on the marine tracker, and typed and retyped a dozen response possibilities. Jonas's words were wistful but never pushy. He didn't ask me to fly to the next port to meet him, and he didn't offer to visit. Our separation had been so practical—he had to move on, and I had to let him.

The draft emails that spilled from my fingers were the opposite: *I wish I were drinking coconuts with you.* Or: *Maybe I could fly into Neiafu.* Or my last one: *Could you wait for me in Rarotonga?*

I pounded the delete key. Of course he couldn't wait for me in the Cook Islands—what was I thinking? I had already delayed his journey to New Zealand long enough, and there was no way I wanted to sail seven hundred miles by myself at the drop of a hat.

But I *did* want to be with him. Bad.

I started a fresh email again. No false hope, but the honest truth.

Jonas,

I ignored my emails because I didn't think you'd write me. I wish you didn't have to sail off into the sunset, but I understand. I miss you—your smiles, your boat, your bed. The coconuts. Reading your emails is the only thing I can recall doing this week. Please send more.

Yours,

Mia

———

OVER THE NEXT FEW WEEKS, JONAS AND I WROTE BACK and forth every day. His emails were longer than mine, his days full of land-based expeditions or the sights and sounds of the ocean on passage. He told me stories of humpback whales, spouts puffing up next to *Eik*, and road trips around the islands.

My emails were mundane, full of boat projects, because that was the only interesting thing happening to me.

Until an email came into my inbox, my business one that managed the YouTube channel. It started with well wishes and compliments on my videos. Then it segued. *My husband and I are looking to buy a boat too, and take off sailing.* Welina *is such a great boat. We looked for a Morgan 45, but the only one in Florida has osmosis damage on the keel. If you ever decide to sell* Welina, *please let me know!*

I'd gotten emails like this before but had brushed them off. I had fought so hard to keep *Welina* in the divorce. At the time, she was my only lifeline, my only hope to keep sailing.

Now, after all the fights with Liam, the loneliness and isolation post-divorce, the bittersweet memories of Jonas . . . *Welina* felt like an anchor dragging me down.

I spent hours poring through my emails over the next few days, and eventually had a list of twenty-two people who had emailed in the last year asking about buying *Welina*. Every day, I woke up with more purpose than I had in years. I sent emails out, contacted a broker, and raised anchor for Tahiti.

THIRTY-ONE

Two months later . . .

I sat at a café in Opua, New Zealand, barely able to take my eyes off him. He couldn't see me—the café was in the parking lot and *Eik* was out on the far dock, the dock with a locked gate and a big sign that said Quarantine. But Jonas was unmistakable out there. He, Eivind, and the man who must be the new crew member they'd taken on in Neiafu, Lovell, were sitting out on the deck of *Eik*, chatting with the immigration officer.

Lila was next to me, vibrating in her seat. While I knew she was excited to see Eivind safely on land—she'd flown from Tonga to New Zealand instead of joining the men on the weeklong sail to New Zealand—she *loved* helping me plan a surprise for Jonas.

We watched as *Eik* pulled away from the pier and motored through the marina.

"Now?" Lila asked.

"Let them get tied up first."

"If you're not careful, Jonas is going to connect to the marina Wi-Fi and book a plane ticket to come see you before we get down there."

I laughed. Lila had been my little helper over the past few weeks, reminding Jonas that booking a flight would only cause additional stress for him and the weather to sail south was unpredictable. He couldn't leave Tonga to sail for New Zealand until the weather was favorable, and who knew when that would be?

Eik settled into her new slip and I had no more excuses. My stomach fluttered as we walked the dock, passing boat after boat, all the cruisers there for cyclone season.

Lila power walked next to me until she caught sight of Eivind on the dock coiling lines. She jogged to him and he wrapped her in his arms, squeezing her tight. I passed them on the dock, letting them have an adorably tender moment to themselves.

Lovell seemed to recognize me, and grinned. He tossed his head back and, with a cockney accent, said, "He's inside, writing the logbook and such."

I climbed aboard and into the companionway. I

had to take a couple of steps and duck down before I could see Jonas at the navigation table to my right. He was bent over the table, writing out the log entry for *Eik*'s voyage. I knew this was a bittersweet moment for him. The last we had talked, he had planned on listing *Eik* with a broker here in Opua. This could be Jonas's final log entry. His frustration with me over the past few weeks had come out in his emails; he wanted to make plans for what was next, but I hadn't wanted to jinx things for myself.

Reaching into my bag, I pulled out a fresh green coconut, husked to perfection.

"I have something for you."

Jonas startled in his seat and gaped at me, stunned and frozen. I held out the coconut and he blinked.

"Mia. *Mia!*" Jonas rose and enveloped me in a hug. I let the coconut tumble down and land gently on the carpet so I could wrap my arms around him too. On the bottom stair, I was slightly taller than Jonas. I bent my head to press into his shoulder.

Jonas pulled back first. "How are you here?" he said, incredulous. His smile was wide, his eyes crinkling at the corners.

"I flew in a few days ago and met up with Lila."

He bent down and picked up the coconut. "You brought this for me?"

"Yeah, I did." I giggled nervously. "You wouldn't believe how many stores I had to run around to find it. Coconuts aren't as plentiful here as they are in French Polynesia."

"Oh, Mia." This time Jonas pressed his hand to the side of my neck and slid his fingers into my hair. He pressed our foreheads together. "Mia, Mia . . ." he chanted in hushed whispers. His hand tightened, and he tugged me in for a kiss that started gently. Our mouths slid together, Jonas pressed into me, and I heard the thunk of the coconut hitting the floor again.

When we finally came up for air, Jonas took a step back and had to adjust himself.

"What about *Welina*?" he asked.

I shook my head. "I sold her. Her new owners flew into Tahiti last month and we closed."

Jonas placed his hands on my shoulders, eyes wide in surprise. "What does this mean? What are you going to do without *Welina*?"

I tilted my head up at him. "Finding you was a good place to start."

He kissed me firmly, once, twice, again and again until I was laughing and he had to move to kiss my cheeks.

"We have so much to talk about."

He pulled me down to sit on the love seat with him. "Tell me everything."

"When you left Moorea, I knew I had to do something else. I was unhappy; I never wanted to sail alone, and frankly, I was angry at *Welina*."

My boat held so many old memories, and while the newer ones—with Jonas—were good memories, everywhere I turned I saw Liam too. "I love sailing, but *Welina* was . . . she was messy. Even selling off or throwing away things was only a few drops in the bucket. I couldn't see a way out that was better. I wondered about getting back into videos too. I have all this camera gear. It was amazing—I made a little video with the action camera: me lifting the anchor by myself, raising the sails, and having a lovely day sail back to Tahiti."

Jonas nodded. "I did watch that video." He stopped and looked away. "To me, it looked like you were going to embrace being alone."

I placed my hand on Jonas's thigh. "It was more of a goodbye to *Welina*, really. But I remembered some of the things Lila had said to me. You helped me gain some of my confidence back after Liam, but so did Lila. And that got me thinking. I made some videos and put them up on one of those teaching marketplaces. I'll be announcing the launch this week."

His smile for me was so big. He picked up my hand and kissed my palm before threading his fingers through mine. "I am so proud of you. You are going to keep inspiring people everywhere."

"Anyway, someone randomly commented that they would love to buy a boat like *Welina*—well, a Morgan 45 anyway. And it reminded me that I *did* get people occasionally emailing me, looking to buy the boat. So I spent hours digging through my emails or comments and found almost fifty people to contact. I got a few offers in, and a local guy came to do a survey and a few test sails, and the new owners committed. I was worried if I said anything . . . Well, I knew we would start to make plans and they all hinged on the closing. I didn't want to say anything to get our hopes up."

"I am so happy for you." He smiled and tucked my hair behind my ear.

I turned the tables on Jonas. "What are *your* plans? Are you still thinking about selling *Eik*?"

"I have contacted a broker here in Opua. Eivind and Lila are going to stay on board for a little while, but then they are flying over to Australia to meet Lila's family and coming back in March to have their wedding in New Zealand."

I tilted my head at him. "But what about *you*?"

He huffed out a laugh and ran his hands through his hair. "I do not know. I . . . I wanted to see you. I thought you loved sailing?"

"I do. It is definitely not about that." I cocked my head and found the courage to ask the big question. "What if we sailed *Eik* together?"

His smile was so broad, his joy so radiant. "Eivind and Lila are leaving for good. It would just be the two of us."

"I know. I would need to either get a job or keep making videos. I suspended my income from the videos, but I think I could start it back up again."

"Do you want to keep making videos?"

"Do you want to keep sailing?" I countered.

"Yes, I would sail with you. As a partner, my equal. If life had given me a sailing woman to love, I would have done that from the beginning."

I tugged myself into his lap, kissing his neck, right below his ear. "So life's given you a sailing woman to love now, huh?"

He laughed when I worried his earlobe between my teeth. "Yes, I love you, my sailing woman. Very much."

EPILOGUE

Four more months later . . .

LILA TRIED TO GRAB FOR THE AX. JONAS GOT TO IT FIRST and held it over his head.

"Jonas!" Lila whined. "Why would you bring me to an ax-throwing place if I'm not allowed to throw an ax?"

"You threw the ax a lot already. Several times. You were not good then, and you will be even worse now."

Lila blinked up at him and pushed out her bottom lip. She also swayed slightly thanks to the glasses of wine she'd had.

Whose idea was this hen and stag night anyway?

"That might work on my brother, but not on me," Jonas said firmly.

"Lila," I said, diverting her attention. "Let's go inside, get some water, take a bathroom break, and then we'll see about ax throwing."

Jonas shot me a look, but I gave him a reassuring smile when Lila harrumphed and weaved toward me. I looped an arm around her shoulders to help steer her in the right direction.

We were on the outskirts of Wellington, at a winery-cum-ax-throwing-range that was the site of the pre-wedding festivities. Most groups were doing wine tastings and carefully throwing axes, thrilled with the novelty of their sunny Sunday afternoon activities.

But not our group. Lila's friends from Australia—Straya, as she kept saying loudly for any Kiwis in the vicinity—were a rowdy bunch. I understood it—they were college friends, and Lila was one of the first in her group to get married.

I steered her into the bathroom first, where she continued to talk to me from her stall. The wedding was the next weekend at a different winery in the South Island, and Lila's parents were flying in this coming Tuesday. This was easily Lila's default conversation topic and had been for the last month.

"Did I tell you she called the venue 'on my behalf'? She wanted to up the guest count. We don't even have that big of a family. Who the hell does she want to invite?"

I made some noises of agreement and hustled her out the door to the bar. The back of the bar was three shelves of liquor bottles, but then the wall above it extended up and up and up to what must have been a thirty-foot ceiling. It was dotted with high-quality electric tea lights—or at least they must be electric; I couldn't imagine someone using a ladder to light every single one. A strip of mirror rose on the wall behind each tea light, and the whole room glowed in warm wood and candlelight.

Lila plopped onto the barstool and I asked the bartender for two waters. "I wish we could honeymoon on *Eik*."

I laughed. "That's not a honeymoon, that's home."

She made a face at me. "Not anymore. I can't believe we're going to move off *Eik* now."

When Lila and Eivind returned from Australia, where Eivind had met Lila's parents, they immediately bought a car and took off on a camping trip around the country, calling it their honeymoon. They still had some items on *Eik*, so after the wedding, they would drive to the boat in Whangārei and pack their things.

Jonas and I were leaving soon. Cyclone season was ending and we were planning to head north again. We had looked at the charts and the weather, and were heading to Tonga. Jonas barely got to see it last year since they were in a rush to move south before the cyclones started up. This year we had more time, and it would be just the two of us sailing from one port to another.

The bartender came back and slid two coasters over with tall glasses of water.

"Thank you," I said as I watched Lila put her mouth onto the glass without picking it up. She slurped at the water.

"You're welcome. She's having a good bache-lorette party?"

I took a closer look at the bartender. "You're American?"

"So are you." She grinned at me.

"Do you know each other?" Lila asked.

The bartender and I both laughed. "Do you know my cousin in Perth?" I asked.

Lila's eyes widened. "You have a cousin in Perth?"

"No."

She stuck her tongue out at me and ducked down, slurping again.

"Where are you from?" I asked the bartender.

"Boston," she said, with long *a*'s instead of *o*'s.

"Seattle."

"Nice. You live here now?"

I shook my head. "Just passing through. You?"

"Same, kinda. I'm here on a working holiday visa."

"Oh, that's nice. I didn't even know those were a thing until I was too old to do it."

She nodded. "Yeah, it's been good to get out and see the country. There's lots to do and it's not too far."

"Not like Straya," Lila chimed in.

"I'm Mia."

"Claire."

"Lila!" she practically screamed. "Claire. Claire. I have to tell you something." She put her elbow on the counter and watched the bartender.

Claire grinned good-naturedly. "Let me guess, you're getting married."

Lila nodded sagely. "But also, you are *beautiful*."

Claire and I both laughed. She *was* beautiful, with dark cropped hair, porcelain skin, and a nose piercing.

"You're beautiful too, Lila. And unfortunately for me, you're taken."

"And I'm straight."

"That's never stopped me before." Claire winked at me.

"She's taken too," Lila said. "We're going to be . . . sister-wives?"

I put my face in my hands. "Lila, no."

"What are we going to be?"

"Sisters-in-law. But not really." Jonas and I were not engaged and we were not even talking about it. As far as I knew, he wasn't even thinking about marriage because he hadn't brought it up since Lila and Eivind's engagement.

"Why not really?" She frowned. "You love him. You *kiss* him. You want to *marry* him." Her lips tipped up and she danced a little bit on her barstool. "I bet you'd even have his babies. Your babies would be so cute."

"Let's try a sailing season together first. We have a boat for a baby."

Lila snorted.

"Where are your menfolk?" Claire asked, eyeing Lila tipping around on her stool.

"Out throwing axes, probably."

A broad man, tanned and handsome, passed behind Claire. I saw his hand grasp Claire's waist, her eyes flicking to the side to watch him walk away.

He swung open a door to a storage room and stepped inside, flashing a heated glance at Claire.

"Who was *that*?" Lila breathed.

"My boss."

"He's beautiful too. What do they put in the water here?"

Claire laughed, then leaned in to whisper, "He's kind of a jerk." She peeked back at the closed door and dropped her voice even lower. "A hot jerk."

Lila gave her sage wisdom. "Hot jerks can be good for some things."

"Who is a hot jerk?" Eivind asked from behind her.

"Eivind!" Lila squealed, and threw her hands up.

Thankfully, Eivind caught her before she fell off the barstool. "Hello, lil Lila. How are you feeling?"

"We're getting married this weekend." She leaned into his arms and he tweaked her nose.

Jonas came up behind me. He brushed my hair out of the way and kissed my cheek. I almost never wore my hair down to avoid shedding all over the boat, but this time it was down and Jonas couldn't stop staring at it.

"How was ax throwing?"

"Tiring," Jonas said. He glanced at Eivind and Lila cuddling on the barstool. "It is nice to be away from the boat for a little bit."

Eik was hauled out on dry land for a month so we could prepare for the next season. Together, Jonas and I picked out a few projects to do—some were necessary, some were not—and worked on them, together. And we filmed.

I published four new videos to my channel, project-based videos that did really well. The courses sold, and we were adding two new modules. The support of my followers had been tremendous, and they welcomed Jonas with open arms. He still worked part-time for the journal, but together we were making enough money to keep going.

"It is nice," I agreed. He tugged at my hair and pressed his lips to mine. We parted as Lila's college friends came in and brought the party inside.

Stepping out of the way, Jonas pulled me into a corner booth. We slid in and both released big breaths. I was finding this entire pre-wedding hoopla pretty exhausting, and it was showing in the way Jonas's shoulders slumped a little lower than normal. I was glad we weren't separated, boys and girls doing different activities in different places. At least this way I could curl up next to Jonas every night.

"Did you have fun with Eivind? Throwing the axes?"

Jonas tilted his head back and looked at me. "Very much."

"What did you guys talk about?"

"In-laws. Eivind is a little scared of his future father-in-law."

"Really?"

Jonas chuckled. "Once, Lila's dad threatened to cut his balls off."

"Oh my God. That's . . . hard-core." I took a sip of my beer. "You don't have to worry about that with my dad. He's almost too friendly with everyone."

Jonas stilled behind me, and I realized what I was insinuating. My heart raced; my tongue had obviously loosened from the beers and celebrating. Where had that come from?

"I mean . . . not that, you know, my dad is your in-law."

Jonas smoothed my hair back. "Relax, Mia, I know what you mean. Lila has been calling you her sister-in-law all week."

"Yeah, she has." A smile crept onto my lips.

He nudged me. "You kind of like it, ja?"

I squirmed next to him and he raised an arm to let me snuggle into his side. "Maybe."

His rib cage expanded underneath me as he took a deep breath. "Do you . . . want in-laws again some-day?" His voice was soft and tentative. I knew Jonas wanted to get married again.

I had thought about it. The past few months had

been busy, but despite all the stresses and trials working on the videos and the boat, our relationship was solid. More solid than my marriage with Liam had ever felt. And Jonas made me want to believe in marriage again.

"I think I want in-laws again, someday."

Jonas relaxed under me, and I peeked up at him to see his eyes closed and a smile on his face.

I sat up and turned to face him. "I think that if we can make it through a sailing season together, there's nothing we can't do."

He turned too, his face inches away from mine, so I could see those arctic-blue eyes of his. "Are you saying," he teased, a grin on his face, "that when we get back to New Zealand, in November, I'm allowed to propose?"

"I mean, you're allowed to think about proposing."

"No, no, I think I'm allowed to propose when we get back. You can sail the boat all by yourself and I will meet you at the dock with a ring. That would be nice, ja?"

I poked his side and he poked me back, making me giggle. Before I could shake it off and move on, Jonas ran his thumb under my chin, tilting my face up toward him.

"I love you," he murmured against my lips.

"I love you too."

THE END

Thank you for reading.
Subscribers to my newsletter get special content:

—a bonus epilogue for *The Hitchhiker in Panama* about the engagement in Fakarava between Lila and Eivind

—photos and stories from my own trip through the islands of French Polynesia

Sign up for my emails at lizalden.com.

AUTHOR'S NOTE

Dear Reader,

Travel can be extremely isolating, and women who go cruising are susceptible to abuse at the hands of their sailing partners. When you are separated from your friends and loved ones and surrounded by strangers every day, it can be hard to escape.

If you or someone you know needs help while overseas, please consider reaching out to your nearest embassy or consulting the HotPeachPages, an International List of Sexual & Domestic Violence Agencies, that may be able to help.

Have you read the series prequel short story,
The Night in Lover's Bay?
See how Marcella met the crew of *Eik* and started on
her adventure. It's available to subscribers of my
newsletter for free. Sign up and get your copy at
lizalden.com.

Reviews are critical to all authors. You can leave a
review for *The Sailor in Polynesia*
at all retailers
Amazon | Apple | Kobo
Barnes & Noble | Google Books
and
Goodreads | BookBub

Also by Liz Alden:

The Love and Wanderlust Series
The Night in Lover's Bay (prequel short story)
The Hitchhiker in Panama
The Sailor in Polynesia
The Chef in the Mediterranean (Fall 2021)

ACKNOWLEDGMENTS

This second novel was a bit of a bear. When I was writing it, I was also revising *The Hitchhiker in Panama,* and drinking water out of a fire hydrant when it came to learning how to be a writer. It was a bit like starting to mix a German chocolate cake and deciding halfway through that it should actually be lemon meringue. The draft that came out was a mess, but my wonderful critique partners, Jenna, Maye, Kyra, and Thea, powered through and helped me reshape it into something that made a hell of a lot more sense.

Thank you to my editors: Tiffany, who continues to coach me and turn me into a better writer, especially focusing on making my characters better people;

Kaitlin, who polished this book like crazy; and Annette who did the proofread.

I didn't think I could love a cover more than *The Hitchhiker in Panama*'s, but then Elizabeth sent me this one.

To my husband, who is my Jonas. You are the best. Six years of being around you nearly 24/7 and I still want to cling to you like a koala.

ABOUT THE AUTHOR

Liz Alden is a digital nomad. Most of the time she's on her sailboat, but sometimes she's in Texas. She knows exactly how big the world is—having sailed around it—and exactly how small it is, having bumped into friends worldwide.

She's been a dishwasher, an engineer, a CEO, and occasionally gets paid to write or sail.

The Sailor in Polynesia is her second novel.

For 100-word flash fiction stories, book reviews, and teasers for the Love and Wanderlust series, follow Liz.

lizalden.com

CPSIA information can be obtained
at www.ICGtesting.com
Printed in the USA
LVHW032107130521
687361LV00004B/328